THE MYSTERIOUS FOUR

MONSTERS and MISCHIEF

DAN POBLOCKI

Scholastic Inc.

**New York   Toronto   London   Auckland
Sydney   Mexico City   New Delhi   Hong Kong**

This book is dedicated to my favorite monsters: Bigfoot, Bloody Mary, the Jersey Devil, and especially . . . Nick Eliopulos, who is a scary-good editor and to whom I owe so much more than a mere book dedication.

No part of this publication may be reproduced, stored in a retrieval system, or transmitted in any form or by any means, electronic, mechanical, photocopying, recording, or otherwise, without written permission of the publisher. For information regarding permission, write to Scholastic Inc., Attention: Permissions Department, 557 Broadway, New York, NY 10012.

ISBN 978-0-545-29982-4

Copyright © 2011 by Dan Poblocki
All rights reserved. Published by Scholastic Inc.
SCHOLASTIC and associated logos are trademarks and/or registered trademarks of Scholastic Inc.

12 11 10 9 8 7 6 5 4 3 2 1   11 12 13 14 15 16/0

Printed in the U.S.A.   40
First printing, October 2011

1

THE BULLY IMPOSTOR
(A ?????? MYSTERY)

When the final bell rang at Moon Hollow Middle School one afternoon in late March, four friends raced from their classrooms, not knowing that a surprise awaited them. In separate parts of the hallway, Sylvester, Rosie, Woodrow, and Viola each opened their locker doors. They were too distracted by the pieces of folded notebook paper that fell at their feet to notice who was watching them.

They retrieved the papers and unfolded them. Inside, written in thick black ink and in the same messy handwriting, were the words: *Meet me on the tennis courts in five minutes. Mickey.* If someone nearby had been listening very closely, he might have heard strange gasping sounds as four mouths collectively dropped open in shock.

Mickey hadn't signed his last name, but everyone knew Mickey Molynew. He spent most of his time making *sure* his classmates knew him as the school bully. And now, he was demanding that the four members of the Question Marks Mystery Club meet him in a secluded area around the corner of the building, where a rusted fence rose high above the cracked green surface of the so-called tennis courts. Where no one could see them from the street. It was a perfect location for an ambush.

Making eye contact with one another, Sylvester, Rosie, Woodrow, and Viola noticed the pages in one another's hands. Without exchanging any words, the four understood that they were all feeling the same thing.

Fear.

Seconds ticked by, and the hallway hustle and bustle began to peter out. After gathering their homework supplies, the four came together.

"I wonder what he wants," said Viola. "It could be anything."

"Like stealing our money?" asked Sylvester.

"Or making fun of us for actually showing up," Rosie suggested.

"I have better things to do than answer to Mickey Molynew," said Woodrow.

"Yeah," said Viola. "Rosie and I have an audition for the school play in twenty minutes. We have to get ready."

The friends stared at one another in silence for a few seconds, glancing at the pages they held between them — invitations to what would surely be a terrible party. No one spoke, but they realized what they had to do. They were the Question Marks, and here was a perfect question: What did Mickey want?

"He'll be waiting," said Viola, checking her bright green watch.

"Let him wait!" said Woodrow.

"What's the worst that can happen?" Sylvester asked. "Hold on, don't answer that."

Rosie sighed. "If we're going to do this, we'd better get moving."

Woodrow rolled his eyes, then shoved his scrap of paper into his jeans pocket. His ever-present key ring rattled on his belt loop. "But he didn't say *please*."

Outside, the afternoon light was making the shadows long. As the four rounded the corner of the school onto the sloped pathway that led down to the courts, a chill seeped through their jackets, sweaters, and scarves. Above, the crystal sky was brushed with feather-light, pink-tinged clouds.

In the center of the courts, a thick boy with a big skull stared up at them through the chain-link fence. He'd shoved his fists deep in the pockets of his brown canvas coat. A purple knit cap hugged his head tightly, hiding his buzz-cut hair and making his ears look even bigger than usual. His mouth was curled up in a pensive, mysterious grimace. As Viola came closer, she pictured one of Mickey's familiar Hawaiian shirts underneath his bulk of clothes.

The group paused at the gate, which was closed and latched. Without a word, Mickey removed one fist from his pocket, then waved them forward. Sylvester glanced back up the incline to see if someone might be watching from a classroom window — anyone who could help. To his disappointment, they were alone.

Rosie flipped the U-shaped latch up, then pushed the gate open. "Come on, you guys," she whispered. "Don't worry. It's four against one. We'll be fine."

"Did you see the size of his fist?" asked Sylvester.

"Show no fear," Viola answered, stepping forward. Then, with confidence, she said, "Hi there, Mickey. What's up?"

As they approached, Mickey stared at the floor of the court. Then, taking a small step to his left, he pointed at the ground. "Check this out."

Keeping outside of Mickey's punching distance, the group gathered to examine what had caught his attention. Written on the ground in fat silver strokes were the words *Mickey was here*.

"Principal Dzielski might be watching from one of the art room windows," said Sylvester. "Are you trying to get us in trouble?"

Mickey shook his head. "If anyone is getting in trouble for this, it's me. Not you."

"Here's a simple solution," said Woodrow. "Don't write your name on school property with a permanent silver marker."

Mickey squinted at him. "That's the thing," he said. "I didn't write my name on school property."

"Well, it sure looks like you did," said Viola, leaning closer toward the graffiti marks.

"But I *didn't*," Mickey insisted. "Not here. And not any of the other spots either."

"What do you mean?" Rosie asked.

Mickey sighed, and his breath clouded in front of his face. He shivered. "Someone has been going around the school writing 'Mickey was here' in all sorts of places. On my gym locker. The globe in Mrs. Huff's geography class. The checkout desk at the library. All of it in this weird silver marker."

"And it *isn't* you?" said Viola.

"That's what I just said! Someone is trying to get me in trouble. And it's working. Ms. Dzielski called me into her office this morning. She said that if she finds one more spot of graffiti with my name on it, I'm going to be suspended. And if that happens . . ." Mickey closed his eyes for a second. "Let's just say, my dad won't be happy with me."

Viola crossed her arms. "What does this have to do with us?"

"Well . . . I heard you guys are good at figuring things out."

"*Things?*" said Sylvester.

Mickey chuckled nervously. "Mysteries. Don't you all have some lame club?"

"Lame?" said Rosie, raising an eyebrow.

"I — I mean . . ." Mickey wore a look of defeat. As he opened his mouth to continue, he appeared to be in pain. "Look, I need to find out who's doing this to me, so I can stop them."

"And how would you do that?" Viola asked. Mickey pointedly cracked his knuckles. Viola shook her head. "Forget it. I'm not participating in something that's going to end with someone getting smacked."

"Not even if they deserve it?" asked Mickey, lowering his voice.

"No one deserves it," said Rosie. "Come on, Viola. We're going to be late."

"Wait!" Mickey cried. "I won't hurt anyone, I promise. I just want . . . I need this to stop. *I need your help.*"

The four traded glances. Sylvester nodded toward the far corner of the court, then said, "We need to discuss. We'll be right back."

Near the fence, out of earshot, they put their heads together.

"I say '*no way*,'" Woodrow whispered. "That guy has practically tortured some of my friends with his threats and tricks and stupid games."

"Yeah," said Sylvester. "Someone is finally getting him back for everything he's done to us."

Viola squinted her eyes. "Even so . . . it's not

fair. Nobody should be bullied, not even the school's biggest bully."

"That's debatable," said Woodrow, crossing his arms.

"Do we vote?" Rosie asked.

"I guess we'd better," said Viola, checking her watch. "Our audition starts soon. I want to be ready."

"Plus, Mickey's not looking too happy." Rosie nodded over her shoulder. Mickey was watching them intensely, as if trying to threaten them into agreement.

"If he wants our help," said Sylvester, "he can relax."

"Then you're voting yes?" Viola asked. Sylvester shrugged. "And you, Rosie?" Rosie nodded. "How about you, Woodrow?"

Woodrow stared at the ground for a few seconds, then shook his head. "He's been horrible to Kyle Krupnik, and if I voted yes, I'd be betraying my friend. Though I guess my vote is pointless now, since it's already three against one."

"I have an idea," said Viola. "This is actually perfect. We can tell Mickey that we'll help him, but he has to promise to be nicer. No more tricks or threats or games. He also has to promise that he won't try to get revenge."

"What do you think a promise like that is worth to someone like him?" asked Woodrow. "How do we know he'll keep it?"

"'Someone like him'?" Viola pursed her lips. "You know, bullies are usually bullies for a reason. He said that he needs our help to make the graffiti stop. He sounds kind of desperate — a good sign he'll keep his promise."

They headed back to Mickey. He wasn't happy to hear about their conditions, but he assured them he'd try to change.

"We'll need to ask you some questions when we have more time," said Viola. "Like, who do you think might have something against you?"

"Try the entire school," mumbled Woodrow.

"What was that?" Mickey said, glaring at him.

"Nothing."

Viola stepped forward. "Can you meet us at four o'clock?" Mickey nodded. "How about at the Main Street Diner?" Sylvester made a choking sound, but Viola continued. "Sylvester's parents usually let us hang out at the corner booth near the front window. Right, Sylvester?"

Sylvester turned red, but he managed to say, "Yeah, sure."

Mickey grunted an agreement, then stomped off toward the chain-link fence. He turned and called out what sounded like *thanks* . . . but it might have been a cough.

Sylvester and Woodrow waited for Viola and Rosie outside the auditorium. When auditions were finished, a mass of their schoolmates spilled

8

through the doors, gossiping about who Mrs. Glick might cast in the leading roles.

"How did it go?" Sylvester asked the girls after they'd made their way through the crowd.

"I thought Rosie did a great job," said Viola. "I can't believe she's never acted before."

Rosie's cheeks flushed. "Viola blew me away. Everyone could hear her clear to the back of the room. And her monologue . . . Gosh, I was practically in tears. It's no wonder though. She's been performing since kindergarten."

"Only little parts in community theater," said Viola, blushing too.

Sylvester nudged Viola's shoulder. "Who knew?"

"I hope you both get a great part," said Woodrow, pushing open the front doors of the school. "What's the play?"

"*The Villain's Web,*" said Viola with a smile. "It's a mystery."

"Speaking of which," Rosie said, glancing at her watch, "we'd better get a move on if we're going to make it to the diner by four."

Woodrow rolled his eyes. "Let him wait," he said. But the other three picked up their pace. Since Woodrow didn't want to be left behind, he had to do the same.

Moon Hollow was a small town, and it was easy to get around quickly if you knew the short-cuts. An alley here, a backyard there, and before they knew it, the Main Street Diner stood before them, the windows reflecting the late afternoon glare off the Hudson River, which was farther downhill. Sitting on the front steps, Mickey stared at the group. Even though they were there to help him, they slowed down and approached with caution.

Mickey stood and tilted his head at the entrance behind him. "This your place?" he asked Sylvester.

"It's my parents' restaurant," Sylvester said, not quite believing he was having a friendly conversation with the boy who had once tripped him in the gym locker room. "They bought it from the previous owner before I was even born."

"Let's go inside," said Viola, taking the first step. "It's getting cold out here."

The corner booth was empty. Viola, Sylvester, Rosie, and Woodrow squeezed in on one bench. Mickey sat alone on the other. Mr. Cho came over to the table, clearly happy to see them. "The usual?" he asked.

"Yes, please!" said the four, while Mickey stared awkwardly at the silverware.

Once Mr. Cho went to the kitchen, Viola mentioned, "We always get french fries. They're the best. You can have some if you want." Viola felt Sylvester nudge her leg with his knee, but she ignored him. "So, what else can you tell us about this graffiti impostor?"

"I don't know," said Mickey, keeping his eyes down. "Woodrow said it himself. Lots of people hate me at school."

Woodrow raised his eyebrows. "You make it easy!" he cried, before he realized what he'd said. Surely Mickey would reach across the table and strangle him now.

But Mickey stayed seated. He didn't even blink. "I guess I deserve it. I just thought . . ." He didn't finish.

"You thought what?" Rosie asked.

"I thought if I was scary enough, everyone would leave me alone." Mickey finally looked up. "Stupid. I know. But now that the principal is involved, and I might get kicked out of school for a while . . . I couldn't care less if that happened, but my dad would be really upset. And you don't want to see him when he's upset. Trust me."

No one spoke for several seconds. Then, as usual, Viola broke the silence. "Well, we'll just have to make sure that doesn't happen." To everyone's surprise, she reached out and patted Mickey's hand.

For a moment, he flinched like an angry dog who didn't want to be touched. Then, he showed a slight smile. "Thanks," he said. "I mean it."

"Why don't you start at the beginning?" said Viola.

"I noticed the first graffiti mark on my gym locker last week. Bobby Grant went and told

Coach that it was there. Coach yelled at me, even though I said I hadn't written it."

"Okay," said Viola, nodding. "So, we already have a clue about the culprit."

"We do?" said Woodrow, concerned.

"Sure." She threw him a questioning look, silently asking him to figure out what she meant. Woodrow folded his hands and squeezed his fingers, thinking hard for several seconds. Finally, he shook his head.

"Is the culprit Bobby Grant?" Mickey guessed. "The kid who told Coach about the graffiti?"

"I don't know for certain, but we can't rule him out," said Viola. "We *can* rule out a whole bunch of other people though. **Do you know who?**"

"Well," Rosie said, chuckling, "we can cross all the girls at our school off our suspect list."

"Wait a second," said Sylvester. ***"Why do you say that?"***

"Where did the graffiti first appear?" asked Viola.

"My gym locker," said Mickey. "I just told you that."

"Exactly," Rosie continued, patiently. "And who's not allowed in the boys' locker room?"

"Oh," said Woodrow. "Right."

"Ha," said Mickey, amused.

"So we know we'll be looking for a boy," said Viola. "But that's half the school. We obviously need to narrow our search down."

"But *how* narrow?" said Sylvester. They all looked at him as if he were speaking another language. "What I mean is: How can we be sure that whoever is writing the graffiti is doing it alone?"

Mickey looked nervous. "I never thought it might be more than one person."

"Detectives have to consider every possibility," said Viola. "And that's a really good question, Sylvester. *If Mickey has made more than one enemy at Moon Hollow Middle School, how can we rule out more than one culprit?*"

"Oh, well, that's easy," said Rosie. "We'll just compare the handwriting of the graffiti. If it's all the same, we know we're dealing with one person. If the handwriting differs, we're looking for a team."

"Yeah," said Woodrow, "but how are we supposed to look at the differences if the graffiti is in different locations?"

"Can you bring your camera to school tomorrow?" Viola asked. "You can shoot all of the graffiti, and we can compare the pictures."

Woodrow sighed. "I think my batteries are dead."

"I've got some batteries at home," Rosie offered.

Mr. Cho approached the table, this time with a steaming plate of french fries. "I'll grab you some ketchup," he said, leaning over the adjacent table. "Oh, and Sylvester . . ." He pointed at his wristwatch. "Homework?"

When the group had finished their snack, they went out to the street and said good-bye to Mickey. "Thanks, you guys," he said. "You're really good at this. I'm sorry I called your group lame."

"We still have a ways to go," said Viola. "We'll see you tomorrow. Tonight, think some more about our next step. You might just solve this one yourself."

"Yeah, right," he said, laughing. He turned up Main Street and clomped away, his heavy footfalls echoing into the coming evening.

The Question Marks went the opposite way, past the familiar library clock, toward the block where they all lived. Woodrow lagged a few steps behind the rest of them.

A strange silence accompanied the group, as if they had run out of things to say. It made Viola uncomfortable. She knew that they should have had questions to discuss and theories to toss back and forth. Having read more mystery novels than she could currently remember, she knew that the answers would only come if she and her friends kept talking. But for the first time ever, Viola sensed that her friends might not be on the same page.

The next morning, Sylvester, Rosie, Woodrow, and Viola met Mickey just inside the school library's entrance.

"The graffiti is over there on the checkout desk," said Mickey. "I don't think the custodians have scrubbed it away yet."

"I can imagine it's probably really hard to get the ink off of the wood," said Rosie, pulling two double-A batteries from her backpack.

"I forgot my camera," said Woodrow. "Sorry."

He didn't appear sorry at all though. In fact, he looked pleased with himself.

Mickey, however, was obviously disappointed. "How are we supposed to compare the handwriting now?" he asked, struggling to control his temper. "We can't wait until tomorrow. If the graffiti happens again, I'm done for."

"I have an idea," said Sylvester. "We don't need a camera for comparison. We just need a little imagination."

"How are we supposed to capture the handwriting without a camera?" asked Mickey. "And don't tell me 'magic.' "

"Not magic," said Sylvester, reaching into one of his notebooks. He tore out a page and held it up. "Only this piece of paper and a pencil." When the others simply stared at him, he continued. "To get a copy of it, all we have to do is *trace* the handwriting. Then we can take it wherever we want."

"Cool idea," said Mickey, impressed.

"The question is, who's sneaky enough to trace it without getting caught?" said Woodrow. "Ms. Newsom is standing right there. We'll never get away with it."

"Like a good magic trick, it's all about distraction," said Sylvester. "One of us needs to pull the librarian away from her desk."

"I can do it." Rosie shrugged mischievously. "Living with four older siblings, I've learned a few tricks myself."

"Then *you* should go ask for help finding a library book," Sylvester suggested. "Once Ms. Newsom isn't paying attention to the desk, I'll swoop in and do the deed." He waved the paper and pencil at them.

"Brilliant," said Rosie.

Once Sylvester was finished, they gathered out in the hallway. Sylvester showed them his work. It was a little messy, but the traced handwriting on his paper was clear enough to get the point across. "Where to now?" asked Mickey. "The first bell's about to ring."

"I'll take this page to the boys' locker room and then out to the tennis courts to see if the writing matches up," said Sylvester. "We can meet during lunch. I should have an answer for you by then."

"What was the question again?" Woodrow asked.

Viola shook her head at him, surprised. "Whether the impostor is working alone or not. Remember?"

The next period, for their poetry assignment, the teacher asked the students to write an ode to spring. She promised to hang the work on the corkboard at the back of the room. Viola sat near Woodrow and Kyle Krupnik. When the teacher wasn't paying attention, Kyle leaned close to them. "I saw you talking to Mickey Molynew this morning," he whispered. "Is he bothering you guys?"

Viola shook her head. "We're helping him solve a mystery. Someone is trying to frame him by writing his name in marker around the school."

Kyle flinched. "You're *helping* him? Why?" His question was directed more at Woodrow than Viola.

Woodrow struggled to answer. "I don't know. I was outnumbered when we voted."

"Mickey promised to stop being mean to

19

everyone if we helped him figure this out," Viola said. "It's for the greater good."

Kyle stared at her for a second, then shuddered. He said nothing before going back to his notebook.

Viola squinted at him. Had she just discovered a suspect? Kyle had certainly been in Mickey's crosshairs in the past. For some reason, his small size made him a target. He might want to get revenge on the bully. For the first time, Viola realized that the Question Marks might have to bust one of their friends. What would happen if that were the case? Would they make new enemies by helping one of their old ones?

The question haunted her for the rest of the morning. Thankfully, at lunch the graffiti mystery itself pulled Viola back into its clutches and distracted her from the dilemma.

At their regular table by the windows, Sylvester presented his conclusion. "All of the handwriting matches up," he said. "You can especially see the similarity in the lowercase a and loops of the e's. We're dealing with a lone artist."

Mickey sighed with relief. "That's easier to deal with than a whole gang."

"Lucky you," said Woodrow.

Rosie lit up. "Hey," she said, "what Sylvester just mentioned gives me an idea about where to head next."

"We need to find a handwriting expert?" Sylvester asked.

"Not quite," said Rosie. "But there is another kind of expert, right here in school, who might be able to help us. *Can you think of who it is?*"

"Sylvester mentioned a lone *artist*," said Viola. "And who here knows about art?"

"The art teacher!" said Sylvester, excited. Then suddenly, he looked confused. "But what can he do for us?"

"What do artists use to make art?" Rosie prodded.

"Art supplies?" said Woodrow.

"And what is our graffiti artist's *supply*?"

"The silver marker," said Mickey proudly.

"Yup," said Rosie. "Our culprit's tool, the marker, might lead us closer to the guilty party. Especially since silver is such an unusual color for a marker. We can ask Mr. Delfin if he knows anything about it."

The group snuck out of lunch a little early and made their way to the art rooms. Peering through the doorway, Rosie noticed that the chairs were empty. Mr. Delfin was sitting behind his desk, drawing in a notebook. She knocked, then poked her head in.

"Hey there, Rosie. What's up?"

"My friends and I were wondering if we could ask you some questions."

"Of course," said Mr. Delfin. "I suppose this is what free periods are for."

Once the group had gathered at his desk, Rosie went on. "In your class, we've used pencils and paint, clay and plaster. But we've never used markers. Do you keep them in your supply cabinet?"

Mr. Delfin gazed at the students in admiration. "I've never had anyone ask for them before. So, no, I don't have any. Would you like me to order some? I'm sure we could experiment with them."

"No thanks," said Rosie, blushing. "But if one of us were to try to locate a marker with silver ink, say, outside of school, where would we look?"

"I'm sure you could find something online," said Mr. Delfin. "But I'd suggest checking Messer's Art Shop on Maple Avenue first. They've got all sorts of great stuff. High quality too."

They all thanked the art teacher before the next bell rang, then headed out to the hallway. "I guess we have another place to meet up after school," said Mickey. "Right?"

"Absolutely," said Viola.

"I can't go," said Woodrow.

"Why not?" asked Sylvester.

Woodrow blushed. "I have . . . something to do," he snapped, before turning and walking away.

"Okay, then," said Viola. "We'll check it out, just the four of us, and let Woodrow know what we find." Mickey stared at Woodrow's diminishing form until it disappeared around the far corner. "I'm sure he's just busy," Viola said, trying to convince herself as much as she was trying to convince Mickey.

After the last bell rang, Sylvester stood at his locker, packing his book bag. He kept thinking about what Viola had said about Woodrow being busy and wondered if that was the truth. Whatever was going on with his friend, Sylvester hoped that he was okay. The Question Marks Mystery Club was supposed to bring them all together, not push them apart. Maybe after this Mickey Molynew Mystery, they'd have to lay down some more ground rules. Maybe a majority vote wouldn't decide whether they took a case; maybe the decision needed to be unanimous. Woodrow obviously felt strongly about not helping Mickey. But after spending even a little time with the kid everyone had called a bully for years, Sylvester realized that Mickey was just like them in many ways. How could Woodrow not see that too?

Sylvester felt a tap on his shoulder. Turning, he found Wendy Nichols smiling at him. Her bright maroon hair was currently cut extremely short, and she'd marked her cheeks with what looked like little eyeliner-made freckles. She wore a floor-length blue cotton dress with a black leather belt wrapped tightly around her waist. Wendy was what some people called "eccentric," but she always made Sylvester smile. "Day-dreaming?" she asked.

"Oh," Sylvester said, chuckling. "No. Just thinking."

"About Mickey Molynew?"

That jolted Sylvester out of his little trance. "Why do you ask?"

"My friends and I noticed you were hanging out with him today." She was able to turn the statement into a question without needing to say anything more. Sylvester suddenly felt the need to explain, so he did. He knew that Mickey had been mean to Wendy in the past, so he tried his best to get all the details right. Wendy listened politely, then nodded. "I always knew you were a nice guy, Sylvester," she said. "Maybe too nice. But you know what they say . . ."

"No, what do they say?"

"Whatever floats your cabbage," she said, closing her locker.

Really? Sylvester thought. *Is that something people say?*

The windows of Messer's Art Shop were filled with colorful displays — paint on canvas, etchings from scratchboard, a messy palette of oil paints propped on a wobbly wooden easel. Sylvester, Viola, Rosie, and Mickey went in together. Almost immediately, a woman approached them.

She was tall and wore angular glasses that made her look like a college professor. A plastic tag pinned to her blouse told them her name was Elsa. "Need some help?" she asked.

"Sort of," said Viola. "We're wondering if you sell markers with silver ink."

Elsa nodded. "Several kinds. What exactly were you looking for?"

"Something that would be nearly impossible to wash off," said Sylvester.

Elsa threw him a suspicious look. "And how do you plan on using it?"

"Oh, uh, well . . . ," Sylvester stammered. "We just wanted to know if you sell them."

Elsa sighed. She led them to an aisle filled with single markers of all sorts — fat, skinny, brightly colored, dark, opaque, translucent, and finally metallic. "Here you go. If you need anything else —"

"Actually," Viola said, "we have another question." Elsa nodded. "Do you remember selling any of these recently?" She plucked a thick silver marker from the wall display.

The saleswoman was quiet for a moment. "I suppose so. But I sell a lot of things here. Every day. You need a name?"

"That would help," said Rosie.

"I do make the customers who want to purchase the metallic markers write their names and addresses in our logbook. You'd be surprised how many kids use them to write on stuff they shouldn't be writing on. Private property and such." She went behind the cash register and pulled out a ledger. She flipped it open and turned to the last signed page. Leaning forward, the group read the name there.

Abraham Lincoln
The White House
Washington, DC
USA

Elsa immediately turned red.

"This doesn't help," said Mickey, fuming.

"But it does," said Sylvester, opening his book bag. He removed the paper on which he'd traced the graffiti from the library desk. Holding it up to the ledger, he showed the group what he meant. The slant and curves of the handwriting were very similar. "Look at the lowercase a. The person who bought the pen here is the same person who wrote the graffiti at school," he whispered to the group.

"And you don't remember what this person looked like?" Viola asked Elsa.

"Come to think of it," she said, "it was a kid. About your age."

"A boy?" asked Rosie. Elsa nodded uncertainly.

"Was he really short?" Viola asked, thinking of Kyle Krupnik. Elsa shrugged.

"Are you *sure* it was a boy?" asked Sylvester, thinking of Wendy Nichols. "Could it have been a girl with short, maroon hair?"

This seemed to confuse Elsa even more. "I don't remember. I'm sorry. But if you write down one of your e-mail addresses, I'll let you know if anything comes to me."

Outside, Viola assured the group that they were even closer than they'd been the day before, but this didn't help Mickey's mood. He looked ready to stomp on something cute and fuzzy. "Let's sleep on it again," said Viola. "Sometimes all it takes is time. We might be missing something obvious."

Later that evening, Viola was surprised to find a message from Elsa in her inbox.

After you left, a memory came to me. A jingling noise. A key chain. The boy who bought that marker had rattled around the store. I'm pretty sure he had messy blond hair. I hope this helps.
All best,
Elsa

Viola felt chills race across her skin. She knew who the villain was, and for the first time in her life, she was absolutely shocked at the answer — so shocked in fact that she kept the knowledge to herself all night long.

Rosie was the first person she saw at school the next day. "Hey, Viola!" Rosie said as she approached from down the hall. "I heard they posted the results from the auditions near the auditorium. Do you want to come with me to check them out?"

Viola was filled with a mix of exhilaration and dread. Still, she answered, "Totally. We need to chat on the way though." As they walked, Viola told Rosie about Elsa's message. She watched as Rosie turned pale, or as pale as Rosie's cocoa skin could possibly turn.

"You don't think . . . ?"

"I don't really know what to think," said Viola. "I also don't know what to do if I'm right. And I don't want to jump to any conclusions or make any accusations without proof."

"But where can you get proof? Elsa's memory seems a little unreliable."

Viola sighed as an idea came to her. "I know what might prove our suspect's guilt. I just need to get something from Sylvester first."

"Really?" Rosie asked. *"What do you need?"*

"The tracing paper," said Viola. "I want to take it to English class. Once I'm there, I'll know for sure."

The girls arrived at the auditorium doors, where a mob of curious students were stepping on one another's toes, trying to catch a glimpse of the paper taped to the wall. Somehow, Viola and Rosie were able to make their way to the front of the crowd. When they read the list, they squealed. Both of their names appeared at the top of the page.

Rosie Smithers — Miss Jessalynn Welford
Viola Hart — Lady Edith Crushing

They'd been cast as the two leading roles! Rosie would play the heroine and Viola the villain. All around them, their peers congratulated them. The girls were so happy, they both felt like they were floating.

As they moved away from the auditorium doors, the thought of the graffiti mystery pulled them right back down to earth. The girls sighed. "Okay, then," said Rosie, trying to temper her excitement. "Where can we find Sylvester?"

The obvious answer was to wait for him at his locker before the first bell rang. When he appeared from around the corner, he hugged them both. "Congrats, you guys," he said, smiling. "I already heard the good news."

"Thanks," said Viola. "But now for the bad news."

In English class, Viola sat at her desk beside Woodrow and Kyle, trying her best to pretend that nothing was wrong. It was easy enough when both boys congratulated her on her role in the school play — all she had to do was smile and say thank you. But throughout class, the corkboard on the back wall kept drawing her attention. The Spring Odes assignment was hanging there, the poems all handwritten individually on lined paper. She kept peeking back at the board discreetly. Neither Woodrow nor Kyle seemed to notice her distraction.

Viola had hidden Sylvester's tracing paper inside her English notebook. She wished she'd had time to check the corkboard before class started. If only she could get closer to it now. Her proof was right there.

As soon as the bell rang, Viola was out of her seat. At the corkboard, she found the poem she'd been wondering about all morning. She held up Sylvester's tracing, comparing the writing on it to the writing on the wall.

She had her proof.

Viola glanced over her shoulder to find Woodrow glaring at her. She felt her face start to burn. She tried to tuck the tracing paper out of sight, but knew it was already too

31

late. Woodrow pushed aside a desk and approached her.

"You can't tell him," said Woodrow. "He'll kill me."

Viola's mouth went dry. She wouldn't have been able to respond even if she had the words to do so. Then, before she could think, Woodrow turned and dashed out of the classroom.

Somehow, each of the Question Marks managed to avoid Mickey Molynew for the rest of the day — a good thing, because they needed time to figure out how to handle their discovery. Back on the block where they lived, Viola and Sylvester met Rosie on her front porch. They knew that Woodrow was in his house on the other side of their shared yard. They'd seen him walk home alone.

"Woodrow is the graffiti impostor," said Viola. "It all makes sense. He never wanted us to help Mickey, obviously, because he knew if we solved the case, he'd get in trouble."

"I'm surprised he didn't resist harder," said Rosie. "Even though he wasn't much help, he still seemed to go along with us."

"He must have known that when it comes to the Question Marks," Sylvester answered, "resistance is futile." Despite the circumstances, the girls couldn't keep themselves from smiling at

Sylvester's comment. "We were bound to solve the case, and he knew it."

"Well, he might have thought that way," said Viola. "Also, he didn't want to look suspicious by completely withdrawing from the investigation. What he didn't realize was that from the very beginning, he was acting suspicious. He said something that first day when Mickey approached us. Before Mickey had even said anything about the silver ink, Woodrow mentioned that it was done with *permanent* marker. Looking back, how would Woodrow have known what kind of marker the impostor had used unless he was using it?"

"What do we do now?" Rosie asked. "He already knows we know."

"And he's scared," said Viola.

"I guess we only have one option," said Sylvester. "We try to talk to him."

They crossed the lawn behind Rosie's house, went around to the Knoxes' front door, and rang the doorbell. Moments later, the lock unlatched, the knob turned, and someone pulled the door open a crack. Woodrow peered out at them. His eyes were red. He was silent for a few seconds, then he choked out, "You don't hate me, do you?"

"Only if you don't let us in," teased Sylvester.

Woodrow smiled, then opened the door all the way. "I had a feeling you all would show up. Come on. I made popcorn."

They sat around the kitchen table, munching giant handfuls of popcorn from the big bowl between them. "I guess you guys want to know *why*?" said Woodrow.

"I think that's pretty obvious," said Viola. "Mickey has been a jerk to you. To all of us, really. You wanted to get him back."

"I stopped as soon as I found out he was in danger of getting suspended," said Woodrow. "I never wanted that to happen. I just wanted him to know what it felt like for all of us. I guess it worked."

"Yeah, but look where we are now," said Rosie. "You've dug yourself a pretty deep hole, Woodrow. How are we going to explain this to him? How is he going to react?"

"Mickey promised not to get revenge," said Sylvester hopefully. "Maybe everything will be fine when you tell him what you did."

Woodrow looked like he might faint. "*I* have to tell him?"

Viola nodded. "It's only fair. Don't you think? That way, you can apologize at the same time."

Woodrow closed his eyes, resigning himself to his fate. "Fine. Let's just hope he keeps his promise."

As it turned out, Mickey did keep his promise. That didn't make Woodrow's conversation with him the next day any less intimidating, especially when Mickey insisted Woodrow tell Principal Dzielski who the real graffitist was.

"How did she take it?" Sylvester asked during lunch period.

Woodrow hung his shoulders, staring at his peanut butter sandwich as if it were the most unappetizing meal anyone had ever crafted in the history of Moon Hollow Middle School lunches. "She was annoyed with me, of course. And she's going to call my mom and tell her what I did. Plus, I have after-school detention for the next week. I guess I deserve it. I'm not a very good *bad* guy."

"I don't think there is such a thing," said Viola. "But at least we now know that just because someone is a bully doesn't mean they're a villain."

"Yeah," said Sylvester. "From now on, Mickey said he's going to try to stop being so mean. And that's a good thing."

"Hmm," said Woodrow, the news finally sinking in. "You're right. That *is* a good thing." He picked up his sandwich and took a big bite. "I'm happy that no one is calling me a bully. Some people might even consider me a hero."

"Well, I bet those people are not sitting at *this* table," said Viola, laughing. Sylvester and Rosie joined in. Finally, Woodrow managed to crack a smile. Viola sat back, enjoying the fact that the mysterious four were finally on the same side again.

2

STEPPING INTO THE VILLAIN'S WEB

All day before her first play rehearsal, Rosie Smithers's stomach hurt so badly that she almost went home instead of meeting the rest of the cast in the school auditorium. Still, she forced herself to show up. When Viola saw Rosie sitting in the last row, clutching at her rib cage, she slipped into the empty chair beside her. She knew exactly what her friend was going through — Viola had felt the same way before many rehearsals back in Pennsylvania. "It's just nerves," Viola said, rubbing Rosie's back.

"I know," Rosie answered. "But if I'm feeling like this now, how am I ever going to get onstage in front of a huge audience? I had no idea what I was signing up for."

"You'll be fine," said Viola. She nodded at the rest of the drama club, who were sitting in the front rows of the auditorium, laughing and chatting with one another. "We're all friends here. Or at least, we soon will be." When Rosie made a doubtful face and clutched at her seat, Viola glanced at her classmates again. "Did one of them say something to you?"

Rosie closed her eyes, not wanting to answer. But since Viola had asked . . .

"Clea Keene has been cast as the lead in school productions ever since first grade. But when Mrs. Glick took over drama club this year, Clea's streak ended. She got a really small part." Rosie winced. "I overheard Clea telling someone in the lunch line that I didn't deserve the role of Jessalynn. And ever since then, I keep thinking that maybe Clea is right. Why was I cast? I've never even thought about acting before you talked me into auditioning."

Viola fixed her jaw and squinted at Rosie purposefully. "Clea's jealous, pure and simple. You got cast because Mrs. Glick thought you would be the best person for the role."

A loud clap rang out from the front of the auditorium and echoed through the cavernous room. "Can I have your attention!" Mrs. Glick stood on the stage. She was a short, striking figure, who easily filled her extra-large orange sweatshirt and black leggings. She raised her arms and stared out at the group of students expectantly. Soon, the cast quieted, and Mrs. Glick was able to continue. "Welcome to the first rehearsal of *The Villain's Web*. If everyone can come together up front, I'll distribute your scripts. Today, we're going to jump right in and read through it aloud. How's that sound?"

"Terrifying," Rosie whispered.

37

Viola squeezed her friend's hand as they made their way down the aisle together. "The only villain you should fear, my dear Jessalynn, is me," she said in the creepy old lady voice she'd used during her audition, the one that had helped her get the part of Lady Edith. "'Everyone else here is just a child playing at being bad,'" she quoted. "'A wise girl would learn to tell the difference between those who pretend to be monsters and those who are truly wicked.'"

Rosie squeezed back, stifling her giggles as they approached the rest of their new cast mates. Thankfully, her stomach had already stopped hurting.

When the girls got back to their block, they found Sylvester and Woodrow tossing a baseball in the yard behind all of their houses. Though the sky was now a deepening blue, the day had been the warmest they'd felt since the end of winter. They hadn't gathered for a Question Marks meeting at the Four Corners — the place where their properties met — in an even longer time. Soon it would be warm enough to return to their original meeting spot.

"How did it go?" asked Woodrow. "Did you win an Oscar yet?"

Viola rolled her eyes, but smiled. "If we were to win an award for acting in a play, it would be a Tony award. Being that our play is not on

Broadway, and this was our first rehearsal, I'd hope you'd have been able to deduce that —"

"I was kidding, Viola." Woodrow tossed her the ball. She caught it one-handed. She nodded an acknowledgment of her awesomeness.

"Once my nerves settled down," Rosie said, "it went pretty well. Everyone was really nice."

"Well, I hope you two aren't too busy to meet with us anymore," said Sylvester. "I was just about to tell Woodrow a ghost story I overheard at the diner this afternoon. I know how much you guys love those."

3

THE PHANTOM IN THE GLASS
(A ??? MYSTERY)

"I was doing my history homework at the counter," Sylvester began, once the four had settled into Woodrow's kitchen, "and who should walk in but our old friend Betsy Ulrich."

"The Realtor?" asked Viola. "Does she still have those crazy blond braids piled on top of her head?"

"Of course. She was the same as always — kooky — just like those ads she posts on the Grand Union bulletin board. She waved at me, then sat at a booth against the wall with a friend — a skinny woman dressed in a black business suit. I overheard Betsy call the woman Carla. She's another Moon Hollow Realtor. Carla was telling Betsy the story of her latest client. It was a weird one."

"*How* weird?" asked Rosie.

"You know the Blackstone mansion down on Marshville Road?" said Sylvester. The other three nodded. One of the biggest homes in Moon Hollow, the mansion stood surrounded by trees on the edge of town. It was impossible to drive

40

by the Blackstones' without slowing down and peeking at the gabled rooftop, the sprawling rock walls, the majestic wooden doors at the entrance. Once or twice, a car had even spun off the road in front of the house, and as a result, rumors had swirled through the area that the place was haunted. "After old Mrs. Blackstone passed away recently, her children had taken a vote and decided to hire Carla to sell it. Not everyone in the family was happy to let the house go, but since Mrs. Blackstone had left equal parts of the property to all her children, the majority vote ruled.

"Carla said at first she was excited to sell the house, but as she began to show it to potential buyers, the experience turned into a nightmare."

"Why?" asked Woodrow. "No one wanted it because it was too expensive?"

"Not too expensive," said Sylvester. "Too *haunted*. One room in particular gave her a lot of problems. It was a bedroom up on the second floor. The room didn't get a lot of light because of all the shade from the trees, so it was already particularly spooky."

"Did people actually see ghosts there?" asked Viola.

"Carla said that every now and again, the people looking to buy the house claimed that they'd seen a transparent, angry face staring at them from outside that bedroom window."

"On the second floor?" said Rosie in disbelief. "Was there a balcony outside?" Sylvester shook his head. "That is so weird. What did the face look like?"

"A glowing, green-bearded man," Sylvester said. "But the really weird thing was, he always appeared upside down."

"Upside down?" said Woodrow. "That's just bizarre."

"Whenever this face appeared, her clients would rush out of the mansion, shocked and frightened. The house has been on the market for almost two months, and no one is biting."

"That's too bad," said Viola. "At this rate, you have to wonder if the mansion will *ever* sell."

"Carla said the same thing," said Sylvester. "In fact, she said that she suspected that might be the point. And that she didn't believe the face in the window was a ghost at all."

"Let me guess," said Viola. "A member of the Blackstone family who didn't want the house sold was playing a prank."

"That's what Carla told Betsy," said Sylvester. "Dennis Blackstone, the oldest son, had set the whole thing up. It was *his* face at the window."

"Either way, I'm confused," said Rosie. *"How did Dennis create the illusion that he was a ghost floating outside the second-floor window?"*

42

"I know," said Woodrow. "Since Dennis was seen upside down in the window, he must have been hanging down from above."

"But that wouldn't account for how he looked transparent," said Viola. She thought for a moment. "I have an idea." Viola stood and went to the kitchen window. Outside, a blue tint of light still illuminated the yard. She pointed at the glass. "There. What do you see?"

"Your . . . reflection?" said Rosie.

"Exactly," said Viola. "You can see outside through the glass of the window. But you can also see my face looking at you."

"So?" said Woodrow. "Are you saying that Dennis was in the second-floor bedroom with Carla's clients? Wouldn't they have noticed him standing behind them?"

"He wasn't in the room with the clients," said Viola. "But I believe he might have used his own reflection to make it appear as though he were staring at them from just outside. All he needed was a piece of glass hanging outside at the correct angle."

Sylvester nodded. "Carla told Betsy that she'd found a large piece of glass rigged up outside the window, hanging away from the house at forty-five degrees. When Dennis looked into the glass, his reflection was visible to the people in the bedroom."

"If that's the case," said Woodrow, "where was Dennis hiding?"

"He must have been directly below the second-floor bedroom," said Rosie. "He simply stuck his head out the window of the room he was in, held a green-tinted flashlight at his face, and . . . *oooh*, ghostly image outside."

"But then why did Dennis appear to be upside down?" asked Woodrow.

"Simple science, really," said Rosie. She took out her notebook and quickly drew a diagram. "Look. If Dennis had stuck his head out the window on the first floor and looked directly upward into the rigged piece of glass, his reflection would appear to be upside down. He must not have taken that into consideration when creating his ghostly persona."

"Ha," said Viola. "Clever. So what did Carla do when she found out who was really haunting Blackstone Mansion?"

"She told the rest of the family," said Sylvester. "They were so upset that Dennis had attempted to deceive them, they won't allow him in the house again until it sells.

"Betsy and Carla chuckled together about the story as my dad brought them the check. As they left the diner, I overheard Betsy mention that she too had once tried to sell a house that people thought was haunted. But we're already familiar with that story."

"Yes," said Viola, with a smirk. "All too familiar."

4

ANOTHER DAY, ANOTHER DRAMA

Having thought about Sylvester's ghost story all night, Rosie decided to share it with her cast mates the next day during a break at rehearsal. Viola sat back and listened. Their new friends sat in a circle on the stage, entranced by the tale of the Blackstone Mansion and the Realtor who debunked the haunting. Afterward, while Mrs. Glick had stepped away to take a phone call, everyone debated whether or not ghosts truly existed.

"Well, of course they exist." One voice spoke louder than the others. Clea Keene stood up, towering over the group. Remembering Rosie's account of Clea's lunchtime cruelty, Viola thought she looked fairly ordinary. Her straight brown hair fell to her shoulders. She wore thick, round glasses. Her wide eyes were the color of ice. "Everyone here should know that, especially those of us who've performed in this auditorium before."

"What do you mean?" asked Viola.

"There's a ghost haunting this very stage," Clea claimed. "The Lady in Green. Lots of people have seen her — a pale apparition in a green dress. They say that if you wear the color green on this stage, the Lady will curse you during your performance. She's quite a jealous ghost."

Rosie gasped. Yesterday, Mrs. Glick had showed the cast sketches of their costumes. Rosie's was a pine-colored velveteen gown. Viola noticed Rosie clutching her ankles. "What kind of curse are we talking about?" asked Viola. She wondered if Clea wasn't the jealous one here.

"Oh, you know," said Clea, waving her hands dramatically. "People have tripped and fallen off the stage. They've forgotten their lines halfway through the performance. Once, I heard that a girl even got a really bad stomach flu. This girl was so superstitious after that, she never set foot in this room again . . . or wore the color green."

Now, Rosie hugged her knees tight to her chest.

Viola leaned forward. "Have *you* ever seen this Lady in Green?"

"As a matter of fact," said Clea, "I have experienced some ghostly phenomena in here in the past . . . when I had a leading role." She crossed her arms. "The ghost doesn't seem to like people who get the big parts. Guess I got lucky this year."

Viola wasn't impressed. "What kinds of things did you see?"

Clea looked down her nose at Viola, obviously unhappy that someone was challenging her. "If you must know, the Lady in Green knocked over my flower vase in my dressing room last year. I was looking in the mirror, checking my makeup, when suddenly the good-luck rose my mom had gotten me simply fell over by itself. I knew it was the Lady who'd done it." Clea smiled. "Then, during that same show, I was coming offstage when I heard someone call my name. I thought it was one of my friends about to tell me what a good job I'd done, but when I looked around, I realized that I was alone back there in the wings. I got the biggest goose bumps ever!" Clea rubbed at her arms as if she still felt a chill.

"Sounds scary," Rosie said. "I'm sorry that happened to you."

Clea shrugged. "Let's hope you have better luck than I did . . . *Jessalynn*."

Mrs. Glick clapped her hands as she came down the auditorium aisle. No longer on her call, now she was all business. "Everyone ready? Let's get back to work."

5

EVIDENCE OF JEALOUS SPIRITS
(A ???? MYSTERY)

The group spent the rehearsal reading through the play again, only this time, Mrs. Glick began to do some preliminary "blocking," which was, Rosie understood, the act of learning where to stand when you said your lines. Rosie took many notes on her script, marking every time Mrs. Glick asked her to move. It was difficult to concentrate, however, because whenever Rosie looked up, she noticed Clea Keene watching her. Clea always smiled in response, but having grown up with four older siblings, Rosie knew a fake smile when she saw one. This made her even more nervous than she already was. She hadn't signed up to become someone's enemy. So when the rehearsal was finished, Rosie approached Viola with an idea.

"Let's solve the mystery of Clea's ghost," said Rosie, sitting on the sloped edge of the stage. "If there's one thing we've learned so far, it's that not every 'haunting' is what it seems. Let's debunk this one so Clea won't have a reason to be scared in here. Maybe she'll even want to be friends."

Viola raised an eyebrow. "If you want to try to smooth things over with her, I'll help you, but I'm not so sure I want to be friends with Clea. I get a strange feeling from her." She thought for a moment. "We do have to get along though. . . ."

"And this sounds like a good mystery," said Rosie hopefully.

Viola smiled. "Okay. I'm in."

Rosie chuckled. "That was easy."

After the last person left the auditorium, the girls gathered their belongings and began to explore. Only a few lights were left on near the stage, and so the space took on an eerie atmosphere. Shadows hid the far corners of the room — cloaks of perfect black. Anyone or anything might have been standing there, watching them. The girls had to force their brains to stay on task.

They wandered across the stage, listening for strange sounds that could have been mistaken for voices. Offstage, behind the proscenium, Rosie discovered a room with electrical equipment. Along one wall was a panel dotted with little glowing lights, indicating the many power switches used to control the elaborate lighting rig that hung over the stage. A stool stood next to a small table. "This is probably where the stage manager sits, calling the cues, making sure the show is running properly," said Viola.

"Huh," said Rosie. "If this is near where Clea said she heard a voice calling her name, someone could have been in this small room. That's who she might have heard."

"Clea said she looked everywhere offstage and was certain no one was around," said Viola. "Not even the stage manager. But I have an idea that would explain how Clea could hear a voice speaking from back here without anyone being nearby."

"Are you saying there really is a ghost in the auditorium?" said Rosie.

"Not ruling it out yet. But my idea has nothing to do with the paranormal. *Can you guess what I believe Clea heard?*"

"Yes!" said Rosie, peering into the electronics room. "In order for a stage manager to call the cues for the show, he or she would have to have some sort of communication device. A headset or a walkie-talkie. If the stage manager had stepped away for a moment and left the device behind, Clea could have imagined that a disembodied voice was talking to her, when in reality it was probably one of the stagehands in another part of the theater."

"Just what I was thinking," said Viola. "Nice work. Ghostly experience number one is solved. What's next?"

"The dressing room," said Rosie.

Outside the door to their left, which led to the hallway, a machine hummed. Both girls knew it was one of the custodians turning on the vacuum cleaner. They felt reassured that they were not alone.

"Are these the stairs?" Viola said, pointing at the stone steps that led down into deeper darkness.

"I think so," said Rosie. "I really wish you'd brought your —"

"Flashlight?" Viola said, pulling open her bag and removing a small key chain light. "You know me better than that, my dear." The white beam was barely bright enough to show the girls their own feet as they made their way down, but it was effective enough so that they could be sure of each other in the dark. They held hands as they pushed open the steel door at the bottom and found a dim hallway.

Upstairs, the vacuum cleaner droned, thumping and bumping along the wall as the custodian swept the hallway.

Thankfully, on the wall inside the door was a light switch. Viola flicked it up, and a harsh fluorescent glow blinked on. A row of five doors was lined up on the left side of the hall. Farther on, the shadows encroached on a particularly dirty and banged-up door, labeled BOILER ROOM. Viola nodded at the doors on their left. "The dressing rooms?" she asked, stepping forward. She pushed open the nearest door and discovered a small space with a mirror and table built into the wall on one side, and a clothes rack along the other. Rosie was the one to turn on the lights this time. The exposed bulbs around the mirror provided a dramatic effect. The girls stared at themselves in the glow, as if they were honest-to-goodness actors waiting for their curtain to rise.

"So this is probably where Clea was sitting when her flower vase tipped over," said Rosie. The room was suddenly very quiet. The custodians upstairs had either finished the hallway or were taking a break. Rosie imagined the ghost of the Lady in Green appearing in the mirror before her, peering angrily out, furious that Rosie would dare imitate her grand color. Rosie jumped up, and the small chair behind her fell over.

"What's wrong?" asked Viola. "Did you see something?"

"No," said Rosie, picking the chair up and setting it right, "but I felt something. Something that might explain the tipping of the vase. *Do you know what it was?*"

Viola thought for several seconds, then snapped her fingers. "The vacuum cleaners from upstairs," she said. The hum had started up again. The custodians were making all sorts of noise, jostling the machine against the walls. "It might have been possible that vibrations from the hallway above us made Clea's vase tip over. With ghosts on the brain, it would be easy for her to make the leap that it was the Lady in Green's fault."

Rosie nodded. "Just what I was thinking too. It *is* super scary down here, especially when you're by yourself, I bet." She headed toward the doorway, almost unconsciously. "Promise me you'll never leave me alone."

"I promise."

Back on the stage, Rosie said, "So it would seem we have some solutions to Clea's ghostly tales. I want to share them with her, but I still have a couple questions."

Viola shook her head. "About what?"

"The curse," said Rosie. "The cast members who forget their lines. The people who've fallen off the stage in the middle of the show. Maybe the Lady in Green is just a story, but we can't discount the fact that some people have had bad luck here."

Viola smiled. "I think there's a perfectly reasonable explanation for people to forget their lines. It's no mystery really. In fact, it's happened to me. And I know it's already happened to you. *Can you think of what it is?*"

"Nerves?" Rosie answered.

"Yes!" said Viola. "That's not a curse. That's just the nature of performing in front of people."

"But what about falling off the stage?"

"We were sitting there earlier this afternoon. *Didn't you notice anything strange?*"

"A strange feeling?" Rosie said. "Not really, except for . . . Oh wait!"

Viola leaned forward expectantly.

"Well, the stage is sloped quite a bit," Rosie answered. "I guess that would make it pretty easy for someone to lose his or her footing and topple into the orchestra pit. Gosh . . . how embarrassing. If that happened to me, I'd never want to show my face onstage ever again either!"

Viola laughed. "Let's put that in our 'blocking' instructions." She pulled her script from her book bag and wrote something in the margins before reading it aloud. *"'Avoid pitfalls.'"*

"That's what I tell myself every day," Rosie said, flicking her hair off her shoulders with enough attitude to rival Clea Keene.

6

A VISIT TO PURGATORY

The next day, Viola, Rosie, Sylvester, and Woodrow went on a field trip up into the Moon Hollow Hills, to a glacial rock formation known as Purgatory Chasm. Eons ago, ancient ice had moved across the land, leaving behind a deep gouge in the thick rocks. Now the park's tall, sheer cliffs and mazelike caverns were a geology teacher's dream . . . or nightmare. Everyone knew how dangerous the place could be, hence its ominous name. One wrong step . . . and splat.

While riding the bus, the Question Marks' classmates were unusually well-behaved, if only because they were under threat of returning to school if anyone acted up — and no one wanted to miss the creepiest field trip of the year.

Rosie and Viola sat in front of Sylvester and Woodrow. Clea Keene happened to share the seat directly across the aisle with her friend, a boy named Paul Gomez, who was also in the play. As the bus rolled out of town and into the forested hills, Rosie had an idea. She hadn't yet gotten a chance to tell the boys about the Lady in Green mystery, and she also hadn't revealed her discoveries to Clea. She thought it was the perfect time to share how she and Viola had spent the previous evening after rehearsal.

The boys were able to figure out Rosie's evidence in the same way that she and Viola had done, clue by clue. But instead of thanking Rosie for dispelling the ghostly rumors, Clea turned bright red.

"I know what I saw and heard," said Clea. "I'm not a liar. Just because you guys don't believe me doesn't mean it's not true."

Rosie was surprised. "I didn't think you were lying," she said. "I thought you'd feel better knowing that the theater isn't haunted. Mysteries are everywhere if you pay attention. My friends and I look for clues and solve them together." She gestured to her three friends, who were watching the exchange with pained curiosity. "It's fun, especially when we discover the truth."

"I know all about your mystery club," said Clea, looking right at Woodrow. "I also heard about what you did: getting some poor boy in trouble by writing his name in silver ink all over the school. What kind of fun is that? It doesn't sound like something a real detective would ever attempt."

Now it was Woodrow's turn to blush. "I've apologized to Mickey. We're friends now . . . sort of."

"Rosie and I were just trying to help you," said Viola, bringing the subject away from Woodrow's scandal. "We thought you'd be pleased that there's no ghost."

Something in Clea seemed to click. She cocked her head to the side and plastered a smile onto her face. But those icy blue eyes revealed a not-so-hidden anger. "Thanks for trying," she said, turning her back on the Question Marks. "Maybe rehearsals won't be so *scary* anymore." Paul smirked, glancing at Rosie from over Clea's shoulder.

Rosie flopped back down into her seat, unable to hide her own anger for the rest of the ride into the hills, except by rotating her head to watch the world pass by outside the bus's dirt-spattered windows.

Once they had arrived at the park, the class was greeted by a ranger who led them on a tour of the chasm. The group climbed down over large boulders, following one another into the cold shadows of the forest. Dark crevasses opened in the cliffs on either side. Rosie wondered what kinds of animals might be living inside. People said coyotes and even bears lived up in these hills. Was it dangerous to be here? The school wouldn't have allowed the students to come if there was any true threat. Or maybe that was the point of the permission slips — parents had to sign them, just in case anyone was eaten. Rosie told herself not to be silly, then slid down another rock, smudging her bottom with dust.

At the foot of the gorge, the ranger explained more about how the spectacular scene had been formed; then the class made their way up a path that wound back up the steep hillside toward their bus. By the time they made it to the chasm's entrance, nearly everyone was out of breath. The ranger thanked them for coming and asked if anyone had any last questions. Someone in the crowd raised her hand. Rosie had to keep herself from rolling her eyes when she noticed who it belonged to. The ranger said, "Yes?"

Clea spoke up, her voice practically at a shout, so everyone could hear her. "Aren't you going to talk at all about Tall Ted?" she asked.

The ranger's face went slack and turned red. He glanced at the chaperones, who all shook their heads in unison. "We don't have time for that right now," said the ranger, gesturing to the parking lot, where the bus was waiting for them.

On the bus, everyone was curious to learn what Clea had been talking about. She looked as pleased as a peacock to have all eyes on her. "I can't believe you guys haven't heard the stories," she said. "My older brother told me the legend."

"What legend?" asked Sylvester from across the aisle.

"The legend of Tall Ted," said Clea, smiling wide. "Tall Ted is a creature that supposedly lives in the caverns underneath Purgatory Chasm. He stands upright like a human, about six and a half feet tall, but he's not human at all. His skin is pale from living underground. He has no hair. He walks with a limp, shuffling along, dragging one foot behind him. But people who believe they don't have to run when they encounter Tall Ted end up sadly mistaken. Tall Ted has the ability to reach out with his long arms and snatch you up, even if you think you're far enough away. His claws extend far, and they're as sharp as razors."

Rosie shivered. She didn't believe the story. This was purely a legend, and she was a science girl after all. However, the tale got under her skin. Maybe Clea was indeed a great actress.

"Where did he come from?" Sylvester asked.

"Supposedly, Tall Ted was born up here in these hills to a human mother who was so frightened by his appearance, she abandoned him in the chasm. He learned to fend for himself and eventually grew to love the shadows and the rocks there. He's so protective of his home that they say if you take a stone from Purgatory Chasm, Tall Ted will follow you home and take something of yours back with him . . . sometimes, they say, he takes the thief back instead."

63

Rosie listened as almost everyone on the bus moaned. She then watched most of her friends pull small stones from their pockets. "Why didn't you mention this before we all got on the bus?" asked Woodrow.

Clea laughed heartily. "You guys are so gullible!" she said.

"So then you just made all that up?" Viola asked.

"I didn't make up anything," said Clea, wiping at her nose. "My brother told me that story. But that doesn't mean it's true."

7

WOODROW'S BIRTHDAY TRIP

That Saturday, the Question Marks all took the train from Moon Hollow to New York City. Woodrow had invited Viola, Sylvester, and Rosie to spend his birthday at his dad's apartment. Once on the train, Woodrow could barely contain his excitement.

The four sat facing one another, gabbing about the rest of their week. Rosie and Viola were getting more involved in their play rehearsal, struggling to memorize their lines while trying to ignore the obnoxiousness that was Clea Keene. Sylvester had been teaching himself some new card tricks, which he shared with his friends. Woodrow had finally finished his detention. Thankfully, whenever he saw Mickey Molynew in the halls at school, the former bully ignored Woodrow, as if nothing had happened between them.

The group had also managed to dig up some more mysteries to share with one another. Now was the perfect time to tell them — cooped up on a train heading south, with at least another hour's travel ahead of them.

8

THE PET CEMETERY MYSTERY
(A ??? MYSTERY)

"This one comes from one of my mom's reporters," said Viola. "Earlier this week, in a town close to Moon Hollow called Jessup's Creek, there was a robbery. A man wearing a black ski mask held up the jewelry store and made off with several diamond rings, emerald earrings, and a couple gold necklaces."

"Whoa," said Woodrow. "That kind of thing doesn't happen too often up here."

"It happens more than we'd think," said Viola.

"Yeah," Sylvester agreed. "Weird people are always passing through these towns. We see plenty of them at the diner."

"The little old lady who runs the jewelry store called the police as soon at the thief left," Viola continued. "The cops showed up fairly quickly. She gave them the thief's description. He was about five foot, five inches tall and wore a green hooded sweatshirt and pale jeans. She told them what direction he'd taken off in, and they hopped back in their cars to chase him.

"Jessup's Creek is a small town. Much smaller than Moon Hollow. There's only one main street, and the direction the old woman pointed the cops in ended at a small overgrown plot of land within a rickety old fence: Jessup's Creek Pet Cemetery. It dates back nearly a hundred years."

"Oh, that sounds so sad," said Rosie.

"And creeptastic," said Sylvester.

Viola went on. "People still use it as a place to bury their beloved and departed animals. In fact, my mom says that on any given day, you might see a freshly dug grave and a new makeshift marker placed on the property.

"The police were pretty sure that the thief had entered the cemetery. So they stealthily made their way through the gate. The place was nearly empty, except for a figure hunched over a grave in the distance. He seemed to be mourning. The officers crept up to him. When he wiped tears from his eyes, he managed to smear dirt onto his wet cheeks, so he looked like a total mess.

"Ordinarily, when encountering someone in such a sad state, I think the cops might have given him the benefit of the doubt. But in this case, they thought they might have found their suspect. *Why?*"

"That's obvious," said Sylvester. "The guy must have matched the old woman's description. He was probably wearing that green sweatshirt and light jeans. I doubt he still had his black ski mask, but that was probably easy enough to toss away."

"Right," said Viola. "And he was the correct height too. So the police had a suspect in view. But they weren't *positive* the mourner and the thief were one and the same. He didn't have the bag of jewels on him. And he insisted he was there to mourn his dog, Lark.

"Sure enough, he was standing in front of the tombstone of a dog named Lark. But there was one major clue that made his story sound impossible. *Can you guess what it was?*"

"I'm guessing there was something about the gravestone in front of him that gave him away," said Rosie.

Viola raised her eyebrows, egging her on for a better answer.

"Yeah," said Woodrow. "The one thing that could give the thief away was the date on the grave. I bet he'd chosen a spot at random — and accidentally stood in front of one of the older graves."

Viola laughed. "Exactly. It turned out poor old Lark had passed away in the nineteen-thirties, way before the man was even born. Lark couldn't have been his dog, so the cops had caught him in a lie."

"They must have been pretty sure they'd found the guy who'd robbed the store," said Rosie. "But where were the jewels? If he didn't have them, where did he put them?"

"That's a good question," said Viola. "The cops took the man into custody. They found his ski mask in a bush near the cemetery's entrance. But they couldn't find the bag of stolen goodies anywhere.

"I told my mom they weren't looking in the right place. He didn't just toss the bag away in order to protect himself. He must have hidden the jewels in a place no one would think to look. That way, when he was free, he could make his way back to the hiding place and collect them."

"But where was his hiding place?" asked *Sylvester.*

"Since the man's hands were dirty," said Woodrow, "I'm gonna guess that he buried the bag somewhere."

"Yeah!" said Rosie. "In one of the fresh graves. That way it wouldn't look like he'd done the digging himself. No one would have thought to look in a spot where a pet was recently buried. It was a perfect plan."

"Well," said Viola, smiling, "I had the same thought. And that's what I told my mom. She contacted the Jessup's Creek Police Department and told them my theory. They found the bag of jewels almost immediately. In the grave of a rabbit named Fluffy. And now that thief is going to trial."

Rosie began to chuckle. The others looked at her funny. "What's the matter?" Woodrow asked.

"With all the talk of ghosts and monsters we've encountered lately, I was picturing a dead rabbit's revenge," Rosie said dreamily. "Wouldn't it just be *horrible* if the bunny's spirit decided to haunt that thief in his jail cell?"

"He'd deserve it," said Viola. "I would never have thought to desecrate a grave like that."

"Yeah," said Sylvester. "But you'd never think to rob a jewelry store either!"

Rounding a sharp curve, the train rumbled on the tracks, emitting a deep sound as if it were chortling in agreement.

9

THE LEGEND OF PORTAL LAKE
(A ??? MYSTERY)

"I asked my mom if she'd heard anything about that Tall Ted creature up in the Moon Hollow Hills," said Woodrow. "But she didn't know anything about it. I was relieved, since I took a stone from Purgatory Chasm. If there's one thing I don't need in my life right now, it's a monster following me home."

"Does anyone really need that in their life?" Viola asked.

The other three laughed. "The tale of Tall Ted was the most ridiculous story I've heard in a long time," said Rosie. "Clea sure has a wild imagination."

"I'm pretty sure the legend is real though," said Sylvester, growing serious. "I've heard people mention a Moon Hollow monster while at the diner. I suppose they could have been talking about Tall Ted."

"But how many of these tales turn out to be true?" said Viola. "Not many. That's why they're called *legends*. People tell those kinds of stories to explain what isn't easily explained. As members of the Question Marks Mystery Club, we can't jump to monstrous conclusions."

"You're right," said Woodrow. "In fact, after I told my mom about Tall Ted, she mentioned another legend that her coworkers talk about up in the Moon Hollow Hills Park." He smiled mischievously, making his friends wait for it. "How many of you have heard of Portal Lake?" When he got confused stares from Viola, Sylvester, and Rosie, he continued. "Mom told me that far off in the woods, deep in a valley away from any of the main roads, there is this body of water that the rangers have given the name Portal Lake. It's so strange looking that a legend has sprung up about it: The lake is a portal to another dimension."

"What?" said Rosie in disbelief. "That's impossible."

"What's so strange about the lake's appearance?" Viola asked.

"First off," said Woodrow, "the water is a bright turquoise color. My mom says it has an almost alien appearance. Second, they've never spotted any fish living in the lake. Third, and strangest of all, there's no shoreline."

"What's that mean?" asked Sylvester.

"It means that if you walk into the water, you have to watch your step, because the ground just drops off a few feet in. Straight down into a blue abyss."

73

"How deep is the water?" asked Rosie.

"No one knows," said Woodrow. "Some say it might be hundreds of feet. Legend says that it's endless, and if you try to swim it, you'll end up in an otherworldly ocean."

"No way," said Rosie. "There are perfectly reasonable explanations for every strange aspect of Portal Lake. The first one being that it probably wasn't originally a lake."

Sylvester flinched. ***"If Portal Lake wasn't a lake at first, then what was it?"***

"It had to have once been a quarry," said Rosie, "a place where people mine out rocks and minerals. Limestone. Granite. Stuff like that. Now though, it's filled up with water."

"That's what my mom said Portal Lake actually is," said Woodrow. "An old quarry. *But how did you figure that out, Rosie?*"

"First of all," Rosie began, "the fact that the ground drops off so suddenly indicates that the rock was carved out. If you've ever seen an active quarry, you'll notice steep cliffs on all sides. It just so happens that the water in Portal Lake rose high enough to cover the tops of the cliffs."

"Huh," said Viola. "Weird."

"Another sign was the color of the water," Rosie added.

"Yeah," said Sylvester, sounding like he still needed to be convinced. "I've never seen a lake turn bright turquoise before. *How did that happen?*"

"Every body of water reflects the light that hits it from above," said Rosie. "The fact that Portal Lake is bright blue means that there are small particles floating in the water — particles that reflect that precise color. The turquoise is most likely the result of minerals from the quarry rock. And the fact that no one has spotted fish living in the water doesn't mean the lake is a portal to another dimension. People would have had to put fish in the lake after the quarry had closed. And the quality of the water might not be ideal to support life. That could be the minerals' fault."

Sylvester sighed. "Sometimes I think we'll *never* find anything supernatural in Moon Hollow. Wouldn't it have been cool if Tall Ted had actually crawled out of Portal Lake and made his way to Purgatory Chasm?"

Viola shook her head. "I prefer my monsters to exist only in my imagination." She thought for a second, then shivered and added, "Actually, I don't even want them *there*."

1θ

THE SECRET OF THE POISON RAINBOWS (A ? MYSTERY)

A few minutes later, as the train came around another bend in the Hudson River, the four caught a glimpse of the George Washington Bridge up ahead. It majestically spanned the wide water, appearing as if it had been painted into the horizon. The train was coming close to Manhattan. But the group knew they still had a while to go. A perfect amount of time for one more mystery.

"You all know my locker is right next to Wendy Nichols's," said Sylvester. "Right?"

"Is that the girl who recently cut her hair short and dyed it maroon?" Viola asked.

"The one and only," said Sylvester. "She told me a story this week that you guys have got to hear."

"Shoot," said Woodrow.

"Wendy's family recently moved into a new house," said Sylvester. "Her older siblings graduated from college last year, and her parents wanted a smaller place. Wendy told me she really likes the new house. Her bedroom is bigger and looks out on the large front lawn.

"Well, something strange happened at her house this past week. Something mysterious."

"This isn't another ghost story, is it?" asked Woodrow.

"How about you tell me what you think after you hear it," said Sylvester slyly. "Wendy said that after the rain showers on Wednesday night, she woke up in the morning and glanced out her bedroom window to find weird puddles all over the front lawn."

"Puddles after a storm aren't that weird," said Rosie, confused.

"These weren't just ordinary puddles," said Sylvester. "They were rainbow colored."

"Rainbow colored?" Viola said, surprised.

"Yeah," said Sylvester. "Wendy says the colors were a great big swirl and really pretty. She called for her mom to come, so she could show her what she'd seen. Her mom was just as perplexed as Wendy was. They didn't know what to think. But Wendy went off to school, and nearly forgot about it for the rest of the sunny day. When she got home that afternoon, she noticed that the lawn had great big dead spots on it. Patches of brown grass had replaced the areas where the rainbow puddles had been that morning."

"So maybe this isn't a ghost story," said

Woodrow. "Maybe it's really about magical grass-killing rainbow puddles?"

"Hardy har," said Sylvester. "Just listen. Wendy's mom and dad came home from work a short time later and Wendy pointed out the dead grass. Her parents freaked out. Wendy's father ran inside to make an emergency phone call. *Who do you think he called?*"

"It obviously wasn't the magical grass-killing rainbow police," said Woodrow.

Viola squeezed his arm. "Obviously not," she said. "But it must have been someone important if Sylvester said it was an emergency."

"I guess the question is, what would make the rain puddles have a rainbow sheen on them?" said Rosie. "It sounds like what happened on my driveway after oil leaked out of my dad's car. . . ." Rosie's mouth dropped open. "Wait. The puddles on Wendy's lawn must have had oil in them. That's what killed the grass."

"Right," said Sylvester. "And Mr. Nichols went to call . . . ?"

"The oil company," said Viola. "My parents get our heating oil delivered by truck. They hook up a tube to a pipe at the side of our house, and it fills a tank down in our basement with oil."

"So then what happened at Wendy's house?" asked Rosie. "Did the oil company mess up somehow?"

"To say the least," said Sylvester. "The previous owners of Wendy's house had an old oil tank buried in the front yard. They hadn't used that one in years and were supposed to have had it filled in with sand. They'd installed a new oil tank into their basement, just like Viola's house has. That's the one the oil company is supposed to fill. But this week, the company accidentally poured the oil into the *old* tank's spigot. The oil leaked out into the front yard, and after the rain, the oil glistened on the puddles Wendy had noticed from her bedroom window."

"Oh my gosh," said Rosie. "What a mess!"

"You bet," said Sylvester. "It looks like the Nicholses might have to have their entire front yard dug up to keep the spilled oil from leaking any more."

"And to think," said Viola, "it all started with rainbows. I guess it goes to show that not all pretty things are necessarily good." Then she batted her eyelashes and tossed her red curls over her shoulder. "Except for *me* of course," she finished, with a guffaw.

11

THE TALE OF THE MEAN MARTIAN
(A ?? MYSTERY)

The four arrived at Grand Central Terminal right on time. Woodrow's dad met them at the big clock in the center of the cavernous hall. Above, painted constellations shone down on everyone, glowing in the afternoon light.

The weather was brisk, but nice enough to walk back to Mr. Knox's high-rise apartment on Fifty-seventh Street. Sylvester had been there before, but the two girls had not. They squealed with wonder at the magnificent view of Central Park from the wide living room windows. The trees were still bare, but the expanse of blue sky meeting the line of buildings in the distance was like something out of a storybook.

Soon Mr. Knox led them back out into the city. They wandered north through the park, to the Metropolitan Museum of Art. Sylvester begged everyone to follow him to see the Temple of Dendur in the Egyptian wing.

"Hey look, Woodrow," said Sylvester, once the four had crowded up into the temple's entry. "They had graffiti all the way back then too!"

Someone named Leonardo had scratched his name into the soft stone, with a date of 1820.

Woodrow blushed. "Not funny, dude. It's my birthday. I deserve a break, don't you think?"

As they all came back down the stairs, Viola whispered to Woodrow, "I thought it was a little bit funny."

Woodrow managed to crack a smile.

Late in the afternoon, after they rode the Ferris wheel inside a toy store in Times Square, Mr. Knox steered the group to Woodrow's final birthday surprise. They crossed Seventh Avenue, and Woodrow released a loud whoop when he saw what was ahead. "Don't tell me we're actually going to the Milky Way Café!" he cried out. "I've wanted to eat there, like, forever!" Mr. Knox simply smiled and led the way.

The front of the restaurant was built to look like an old-fashioned diner that had been modified into a giant silver rocket ship aimed at the sky. Inside, two uniformed space officers greeted the group and brought them upstairs to a booth that resembled a space station escape pod. A wide circular table illustrated with a red Martian landscape stood between them. Flat screen monitors in the walls gave the illusion that they were racing through a streak of stars at warp speed, and eerie music from science fiction films floated in the air. Woodrow and his friends were impressed.

When their waiter showed up, Rosie nearly screamed. He towered over the table in a Martian costume. He wore the same uniform as the officers downstairs, but his head was large, bulbous, and green. Big black eyes stared blankly out at them, and an electronically modified voice asked in a high-pitched whine, "Can I get you anything to slurp on?"

They all laughed, then ordered Cokes.

There were different kinds of alien waiters. Some looked like demons, some like shimmery humans. And at least one resembled their own green Martian, only theirs was taller. When he — *it* — came back with their drinks, they ordered food. Woodrow couldn't resist ordering the Meteor and Chicken Pie. Sylvester was tempted by the Rings of Saturn Pasta dish. Rosie was curious about Milky Way Soup. And Viola knew what she wanted as soon as she saw it on the menu: the Spicy Solar Flare Salad.

They had a great time. Woodrow was so pleased, he was able to forget about his poor judgment with Mickey Molynew for the first time in weeks. The group finished the meal with Dark Side of the Moon Cake, birthday candles, and that old familiar song.

Afterward, their waiter left the check. Mr. Knox took out his wallet and laid down cash. Everyone thanked him profusely, then stood to go. Immediately, the Martian waiter appeared and took the check from the table, almost poking Mr. Knox in the eye with its antenna. "Thank you for flying with us tonight," it said with its strange electronic whine.

"No, thank *you*," said Woodrow. "This was a blast."

The group went downstairs. Just as Mr. Knox was reaching for the door, someone called out to him loudly. "Excuse me, sir!"

They turned around and found the Martian waiter chasing them down the stairs.

"Yes?" said Mr. Knox. "Is there a problem?"

"You need to pay the bill before you leave the restaurant. That's how it usually works." The Martian towered over Mr. Knox, and even with its silly voice, it clearly sounded annoyed.

"I paid the bill," said Mr. Knox, sounding annoyed himself. "You may remember me handing you the money?"

In response, the Martian simply held up the small black folder that contained their check. The cash, however, was not there.

"I swear I put the money inside that folder and handed it back to you," said Mr. Knox, turning red.

"Then where's the money now?" asked the Martian.

"I think I know," said Woodrow. "Dad, you handed the check to a Martian. But apparently it wasn't our waiter."

"What do you mean?" asked his dad.

"There was another Martian waiter up there. You must have given it to him instead. I thought there was something different about the waiter who took the check." He turned toward his friends. *"Did you guys notice the difference?"*

"Yeah," said Sylvester. "Come to think of it, the Martian who took the check was much shorter than this one." He nodded at the perplexed-looking alien standing before them.

The Martian reached up and grabbed at its head. With a swift yank, it pulled off its mask, revealing a young man with bangs plastered to his forehead. He turned and shouted at a man standing off near the staircase. "Jeff! Sal did it again!"

Jeff, a short, squat man dressed all in black, approached them. He wore a tag on his shirt that read: Captain. Mr. Knox, Woodrow, and the waiter explained what had happened. Jeff simply blinked, then snapped his fingers at the two space officers near the front door. He waved his thumb up the stairs, as if to say, "Put Sal in the ship's holding cell." Finally, he smiled at the group. "Sorry about the mix-up, folks. We've got some rogue aliens on board. This isn't the first time our friend Sal has been accused of something like this. But I'll make sure this never happens here again."

"No harm done," said Mr. Knox. "I just hope the right Martian gets to keep the tip."

$1\text{\scriptsize 2}$

TALL TED TALES

Exhausted but enthused from their trip to New York City, the Question Marks settled easily back into the routine of the school week. Now that Woodrow was done with detention, he and Sylvester met in their yards every afternoon to catch up on their Frisbee-throwing skills. Every now and again, a cold spring wind would lift the disk and send it flying out of reach, but having felt cooped up inside for much of the winter, the boys didn't mind chasing it across the borders of the girls' yards.

Viola and Rosie spent many days after class working with Mrs. Glick and the rest of the *Villain* cast, working to make their scenes just right. Rosie thought it was weird that onstage Viola had become her worst enemy, because off-stage, she was pretty sure they had become best friends.

Later that week, the four finally had a chance to catch up. Since the evenings still left the Four Corners too chilly, the group followed Sylvester downstairs into his basement bedroom. Sylvester's grandmother, Hal-muh-ni, called to them from the kitchen, asking if anyone wanted hot tea.

"Thanks," said Sylvester, "but we're fine."

"I've been hearing weird rumors going around school," said Viola, sitting on the new rug next to Sylvester's bed.

"What kind of rumors?" asked Woodrow.

"Remember that story Clea Keene told on the bus home from Purgatory?" said Viola. "The one about Tall Ted?" The other three nodded. "Well, kids have been saying they've seen him here. In Moon Hollow."

"That's crazy," said Woodrow. Sitting on Sylvester's bed, he sat up straight and pulled his feet onto the mattress, as if something underneath might reach out and grab his ankles. "Right? Tall Ted is just a tall tale."

"I heard something about it too," said Sylvester. "Dale Fichner found strange tracks out on the sports field earlier this week. He said it looked like some kind of animal had limped across the grass, clawing up the ground every few steps."

"That's odd," said Viola. "Clea did say that Tall Ted supposedly walks with a limp."

"It could have been a hurt animal," said Rosie. "We've got foxes in these woods. And I've heard that sometimes bears come down from the hills."

"True," said Viola. "Just thought I'd mention it since some of our classmates are scared. They regret taking stones from Purgatory Chasm. Everyone thinks the stones are cursed, and no one wants to think about Tall Ted showing up in their bedroom at night" — Viola made her voice deep and added — "reaching out for them with his long, razor-sharp claws. . . ."

"That's just dumb," said Sylvester, clutching his knees. "There's no such thing as curses." He stared at his friends unsurely. "Is there?"

13

A CASE OF BAD LUCK
(A ?? MYSTERY)

"I didn't mean to freak you out," said Viola. Her friends all scoffed. "Okay, so maybe I did, a little. Mostly, I wanted to share the rumors so we'll keep our eyes open, just in case there's a mystery creeping up on us. Speaking of which, I've got another one from my mom."

"Thank goodness," said Rosie, wide-eyed. She looked almost as frightened as Sylvester. "This isn't a scary one, is it?"

"Not *scary*, exactly," said Viola. "Although I'm sure some people might find this story disturbing."

"Let's hear it," said Woodrow, leaning forward with anticipation.

"Okay," said Viola. "My mom is writing an article about this for the paper. Recently, a man bought a lottery ticket a few towns away from here. He and his wife had been struggling for a little while to make ends meet. With their new baby, they barely had any extra money, but he still drove his busted old car to pick up a ticket at the convenience store, hoping to turn his luck

92

around. Oddly, he was able to do just that. He ended up winning!"

"No way," said Sylvester, astonished. "That actually happens?"

"They say *someone's* gotta win," said Rosie.

"How much?" asked Woodrow.

"I don't remember the exact amount," said Viola. "But it was enough that the man immediately started getting phone calls from family members he had never even heard of, all asking him for money.

"The man started to get paranoid that one of his family members would find a way to steal the ticket. He borrowed a clunky old safe from a neighbor and locked that ticket up inside. Then he and his wife packed up their car, placed the heavy safe on the rusty floor in the backseat, and headed out to the nearest lottery claim center. They left their baby at home with a sitter, because they didn't think the car was safe enough to drive long distances with their child. On the way to the lotto center, the man mentioned that the first thing they'd buy was a new car. His wife was relieved that she wouldn't have to worry about getting into an accident in their old clunker anymore. They didn't make any stops along the way, because there was always a chance that if they turned the engine off, it wouldn't turn on again.

"When they pulled into the claim center's

parking lot, the couple got the shock of their life. Looking in the backseat, they discovered that the safe was missing!"

"No way!" said Woodrow. "Did one of the man's family members manage to steal it?"

"How would that be possible?" asked Rosie. "The man put the safe in the back, got in the front seat, and drove without stopping. *How would anyone have had the chance to steal the safe from him?"*

"That would have been impossible," said Viola. "No. When the man looked in the backseat, he knew he hadn't been robbed. Because instead of finding the safe there, he found something else in its place." The other three looked thoroughly confused. Viola smiled. *"Do you have any idea what it was he found?"*

Woodrow shook his head. "The only thing I can think of would be a giant hole!"

"A hole?" said Sylvester. "But how?"

"Viola said the car was rusted," said Woodrow. "If the safe was heavy enough, I can imagine that any serious bump might have broken the floor away. The safe could have fallen out on the highway, and the couple might not have noticed."

"Strange but true," said Viola sadly.

"Oh no," said Rosie. "That's terrible!"

"Panicked, the couple backtracked the way they'd come, looking all over for the safe that had fallen through the hole in their car. But it was nowhere to be found."

"Maybe someone picked it up," Rosie suggested. "Maybe they'll come forward with it. Maybe your mom's article will help the couple locate the safe. And the ticket."

"Whoever found it would have to be an especially good Samaritan," said Woodrow.

"That's what everyone at the newspaper hopes," said Viola.

Rosie shook her head. "And to think, if they'd just stuck the ticket in an envelope and put it in the glove box, they'd probably be totally rich right now."

"Just goes to show that sometimes you can be *too* safe," said Sylvester.

14

THE TRICK OF THE UNLIKELY ACCOMPLICE
(A ?? MYSTERY)

"I should probably get home soon," said Rosie. "I have some studying to do."

"You can't leave before you hear the story Hal-muh-ni told me when I got home from school today," said Sylvester. Rosie shrugged and settled down again. "This afternoon, Hal-muh-ni took my little sister out to a park across the river in Highcliff. Since it was a sunny day, there were quite a few people out and about, enjoying the big playground they have there. Lots of baby carriages with mommy purses hanging on the handlebars. A few toddlers wandering around. Gwen and my grandmother fit right in.

"Hal-muh-ni came upon a big crowd gathered near some of the topiary animals. A white-faced clown was doing a mime routine. Pretending to be stuck in an invisible box. Walking on an invisible tightrope. Lifting very heavy invisible objects. Gwen was instantly fascinated, so they stopped to watch.

"The clown eventually motioned for a volunteer. He happened to pick my grandmother out

97

of the crowd. Silently, he indicated that he wanted Hal-muh-ni to open her pocketbook and give him some cash. She knew it was part of a magic trick, so she went ahead and took out a dollar. She handed it over, and before she knew it, the clown had made the money disappear seemingly into thin air. Although Hal-muh-ni had seen me do a version of that trick, she was still impressed. After a few seconds, the clown managed to make my grandmother's money reappear. He did a few more tricks, finishing up by releasing a couple of doves from inside his long black coat. All the kids were surprised and excited. The clown took a bow, then put out his hat to collect tips.

"The audience went for their purses and wallets. But when two women grabbed their purses from their carriages and searched for their cash, they realized that they'd been robbed. Their money was missing."

"Did your grandmother mention anyone suspicious looking lurking around?" Woodrow asked.

"I don't think so," said Sylvester. "And the two women were standing in completely different areas. That's why, when one of them suggested that the clown had performed a trick to make their money disappear, people in the crowd agreed with her. They'd seen him pull the stunt on my grandmother, and now they thought he'd done the same to them. And they were mad that he wouldn't admit to it."

Viola shook her head. "To do a disappearing trick, I'd assume the clown would have had to be up close to the victim. That's why he pulled your grandma out of the crowd. Unless he was using real magic, I don't think he could have stolen money from anyone else in the audience — much less two people standing in two different spots."

"Unless he was using an accomplice," said Rosie.

"My grandmother didn't think he was using an accomplice," said Sylvester. "In fact, she didn't think the clown was guilty at all. There was something about the victims that clued her in. Something they had in common. *Do you know what it was?*"

"They were both moms?" said Woodrow.

"They weren't *necessarily* moms," said Viola, "but Sylvester mentioned that they both had baby carriages with them. That's what they had in common." Sylvester nodded. "But what would that have to do with the clown's guilt?"

"The clown wasn't close to the carriages, where the purses were hanging," said Sylvester. ***"But who was?"***

Viola, Woodrow, and Rosie glanced at one another as the answer came to them. "The kids!"

Sylvester smiled. "That's what Hal-muh-ni noticed. She'd seen a couple of the toddlers reaching into some of the bags, looking for treats or toys or something, when their parents weren't watching. As the crowd started getting more riled up, demanding that the clown empty his pockets, my grandmother went up to one of the victims. She asked her to check her son's pockets. The woman was taken aback. But when she searched her precious baby, she found a wad of cash stuck in his pants!"

Viola laughed. "Wow, they're starting early in Highcliff."

"Of course, the kid didn't realize that what he'd done was wrong," said Sylvester. "Today, he got his first lesson in making things disappear. If he wants to grow up to be a magician, he's going to have to get a lot better at it."

"Yeah," said Woodrow, "and I bet that clown will think again before performing for such a difficult audience."

*1*5

ANOTHER MYSTERY CLUB

A few days later, Viola was coming out of the girls' bathroom when she felt someone grab her arm. When she turned, Viola was shocked to find Rosie clutching her sleeve.

"Oh my goodness, Viola," said Rosie, panicked, "have you heard?"

"No! What?" Viola reeled. Had Principal Dzielski been kidnapped? Did the old Reynolds house finally collapse? Were they giving away free ice cream in the cafeteria?

"Clea Keene is starting her own mystery club!" Rosie proclaimed.

Viola felt as though she'd been knocked against the wall. All of her "let's give Clea a chance" feelings suddenly vanished. "She doesn't even like mysteries."

"Well, she says she does. She's also mentioned that she thinks the Question Marks Mystery Club hasn't been dependable lately and that someone else needs to stand up for the students of Moon Hollow Middle School."

"What's she talking about?"

Rosie simply raised an eyebrow.

"The thing with Mickey and the graffiti?" Viola asked. Rosie nodded. "Granted, that wasn't a nice thing for Woodrow to do, but he came clean. And we *did* get Mickey to change."

"But she's telling everyone that Woodrow changed in the process. She's calling *Woodrow* a bully. And now, she says, the Question Marks can't be trusted. If she keeps this up, people might start to believe her."

"Not if I can help it."

"We've got to tell the boys," said Rosie. "How long 'til lunch?"

About an hour later, the girls caught up with Sylvester and Woodrow at their favorite bench near the cafeteria window. As it turned out, Woodrow had already heard the story . . . and more.

"The others who joined Clea's group are Paul Gomez, Shanti Lane, and Thomas Kenyon," Woodrow explained.

"Another mysterious four," said Viola with a scowl.

"Paul's in the play with us," said Rosie.

"According to Clea," said Woodrow, "each of them has been the victim of a recent crime."

"Really?" said Sylvester. "What crime? How come we haven't heard of it?"

"They've all had something stolen from their houses," said Woodrow. "We haven't heard of it because they hadn't told anyone until now."

"That doesn't make any sense," said Viola. "If they hadn't told anyone, then how did they end up learning that they had this in common? It certainly hasn't made the papers."

"I don't know or care how Clea Keene operates," said Woodrow. "She hasn't been the nicest person to me lately."

"To any of us," said Sylvester. "Ever since Viola and Rosie joined the drama club —"

"That's exactly it," said Viola. "Clea doesn't care about mysteries. But she *does* care about how much attention she gets. Since she's not the lead in the school play this year, she needs something else to concentrate on."

"But Moon Hollow mysteries already belong to *us*," said Sylvester, angrily chewing his sandwich. He nearly spit a piece of it out onto the table.

"Mysteries don't really *belong* to anyone," said Woodrow. He sat back and crossed his arms. "Let Clea and her friends do what they want. Since they're a so-called mystery club now, they can figure out who robbed them on their own. We'll concentrate on other things."

"Yeah . . . other things," said Rosie, trying to sound perky, "like the story my mom told at dinner last night."

16

THE MYSTERY OF THE SHRUNKEN MONEY
(A ???? MYSTERY)

"Mom came home from work looking really frustrated," said Rosie. "My family thought she'd just had another busy day at the library, but at dinner, when my oldest sister, Grace, asked her what was wrong, Mom reached into her pocket and pulled out a twenty-dollar bill. Grace's face lit up as my mom held it out to her. The rest of my brothers and sisters were disappointed that they hadn't thought to comfort my mother first. But they didn't understand that Mom wasn't rewarding Grace. She was simply showing her why she was frustrated."

"Why would a twenty-dollar bill make your mom upset?" asked Sylvester.

"None of us knew why until Mom took out two more twenties. She handed these to Grace as well. My sister looked like she had won the lottery — until my mom asked her to compare them. Confused, Grace held up the three bills. She immediately noticed the difference between them. The first bill was a tiny bit smaller than the other two."

"How is that possible?" asked Woodrow. "Did it shrink in the wash?"

"No, it didn't shrink in the wash," said Rosie, chuckling. "But that was a good guess. I suppose the answer to your question lies inside another question. *Why would my mom be upset that one of her twenties was smaller than the others?*"

"I know why," said Viola. "Because that means she can't spend the first bill."

"Why not?" said Sylvester. "Just because one bill is smaller than the other, doesn't mean they aren't worth the same."

Viola shook her head. "Actually, that's exactly what it means. They aren't worth the same at all. Right, Rosie?"

Rosie nodded. *"Can you guys figure out why?"*

"Every piece of American paper currency is the exact same size," said Woodrow. "So if one twenty-dollar bill was a smaller size than the others, that means the bill was a fake."

"A fake?" said Sylvester, impressed. "You mean, like counterfeit money?"

"Exactly," said Rosie. "Mom was upset because she'd gone to the pharmacy to pick up some stuff after work. She paid the cashier with a one-hundred-dollar bill and got a lot of change back, including that twenty. Then she went next door to the grocery store. She picked up food for dinner, but when she went to pay, the grocery store cashier wouldn't accept her money."

"Let me guess," said Viola. "The cashier noticed the smaller size of the twenty, and realized it was a fake?"

Rosie nodded. "My mom was able to pay with her debit card, but she still left the store angry and embarrassed. She immediately went back to the pharmacy to show the fake bill to the store manager. After a brief discussion, the manager brought over the cashier who had helped my mom earlier. My mom was about to shrug it off and call the whole thing an honest mistake, when suddenly the cashier got really defensive. He said that my mom was trying to swindle the store and get him in trouble. My mom was so shocked, she didn't even know what to say. The manager didn't know what to believe, and so he

108

did nothing. More frustrated than ever, my mother left the store with the fake bill stuck in her pocket.

"My mom said she wouldn't have noticed the difference in the money if the grocery store clerk hadn't pointed it out to her. She wondered why the pharmacy cashier had become so defensive, when clearly, it was an easy mistake to make. I immediately thought of an answer. *Can you?"*

"It wasn't a mistake at all," said Woodrow. "The pharmacy cashier gave your mom that fake bill on purpose."

"But what would giving a fake bill to Mrs. Smithers accomplish?" Sylvester asked. *"Was the pharmacy cashier just being mischievous?"*

"I'd say he was more devious than mischievous," said Viola. "He'd just stolen from Rosie's mom, after all."

"Stolen?" said Sylvester.

"By giving Mrs. Smithers a *fake* bill, the cashier had basically added an extra twenty dollars to his register — the real twenty-dollar bill that was supposed to go to Rosie's mom," said Viola. "How easy would it be for the cashier to stick that extra twenty in his pocket later?"

"Pretty easy," said Woodrow.

"That is so sneaky!" said Sylvester.

"And totally illegal," said Rosie.

"So what's your mom going to do about it?" Sylvester asked.

Rosie shrugged. "There's nothing she really can do. The cashier cashed in — this time. But my mom said she takes comfort in knowing no one gets away with that kind of thing for long. Bad behavior always comes back to bite."

17

THE HORROR IN THE DRESSING ROOM

When classes finished, Viola and Rosie met the rest of the *Villain* cast in the auditorium. Instead of calling the group to the stage for a warm-up, Mrs. Glick told everyone that the costume co-coordinator, a broad-shouldered and square-jawed young man named Joey, had arrived to test out some of the outfits they would wear during the show. Joey called several members of the group at a time to come into the wings and search the clothing racks for the costumes he'd brought them. Soon, it was Viola and Rosie's turn. Joey handed the girls a couple of frilly, Victorian-looking dresses and pointed down the stairs to the dressing room hallway. Rosie carried her green gown with trepidation, remembering Clea's ghost story about the Lady in Green's curse. Even though the Question Marks had successfully debunked Clea's claims, Rosie couldn't help but worry about the ghost.

Downstairs, the girls found most of the dressing rooms being used by the boys in the cast. Near the end of the hall, where the fluorescent lights flickered weakly, they located a room where a few of the girls were changing. Unfortunately, the one person they didn't wish to see greeted them as soon as they stepped through the door.

"Well look who it is," said Clea. "The stars of the show."

Viola and Rosie said hi to everyone, then moved off to a private corner.

"I'm glad you two are here," Clea continued. "I was just telling the others about my new mystery club. We're called the Question Troop."

"The Question Troop?" Viola said, turning red. "That's almost exactly the same as —"

"We heard all about it," said Rosie, squeezing Viola's shoulder. She forced herself to smile.

"Oh, good," said Clea with barely concealed pleasure. "Word is spreading. I suppose if anyone in our class needs help solving a mysterious occurrence, they'll come straight to us."

"How nice for you," said Viola, through gritted teeth.

Rosie worried that things were starting to get ugly. She didn't want to give Mrs. Glick a reason to expel anyone from the cast. "Did you guys figure out who stole your stuff yet, Clea?" Rosie asked.

Clea glared at Viola. "We're working on it. Closer and closer. Paul believes that it's someone who's good at being tricky, maybe even someone we know." She plucked a piece of fuzz off her lapel and flicked it away. "If there's something

113

we've all learned recently, it's that the villain might be the person you'd never suspect. He might even be one of your closest friends."

Out in the hallway, someone started screaming. Clea's eyes went wide, and even though she stood closest to the door, she froze and simply stared at it. But Viola sprang into action. She dashed forward, clutched the knob, and swung the door open.

Evan Gleeson was huddled against the far wall. He was staring down the hallway, where the fluorescent lights had given out and darkness had taken over. He looked like he'd seen the Lady in Green herself. "What's wrong?" Viola asked.

At the sound of her voice, Evan snapped out of it. "T-Tall Ted," he stammered. "I think I saw him down there in the dark. He limped away from me and went through the door to the boiler room." Soon, the other boys in the cast crept up behind Evan, looking curious and a little shocked. "I knew I shouldn't have taken one of those stones. He came to take it back from me!"

"Shh," Viola said. "We don't want to scare him away."

"Scare *him* away?" said Evan.

Viola felt someone push by her. Clea was walking steadily down the hall toward the boiler room door. "Come on, you guys. The Question Troop is on the case."

Rosie came up beside Viola. Glancing at each other, they didn't have to speak to know that they weren't going to let Clea beat them to the punch. They took off after her. Some of the cast followed.

When they arrived at the boiler room, Clea slowly reached out to open the door. A musty smell crept out of the pitch-black room. If there was a light inside, no one knew where to find the switch. "Shoot," said Viola. "I left my flashlight upstairs."

"Hello?" Clea called into the darkness. "Who's in here?"

For a few seconds, there was only silence. Then, to everyone's surprise, a low growl echoed out into the hallway. The group froze as the sound grew louder and higher. A scraping sound moved around inside the veil of black. Rosie imagined toenails dragging on concrete.

Someone in the group screamed. Someone else slammed the door. Then, like a flock of nervous birds moving all at once, the entire cast of *The Villain's Web* raced back to the stairwell and up to the stage.

Joey, the costume co-coordinator, found them crowded together backstage. Evan told Mrs. Glick what he'd seen. Mrs. Glick and Joey went down to explore, but they found nothing unusual.

After the hubbub died down, Joey offered to escort the cast downstairs so they could collect the costumes from the dressing rooms. Mrs. Glick promised everyone that they had only allowed their imaginations to get the best of them. When the cast made it back up to the stage, the director asked them to sit in a circle and take out their scripts.

Clea's friend Paul Gomez reached into his backpack, then let out a yelp. Everyone jumped. "Someone stole my wallet!" Paul cried. "It was in the front pocket earlier. And now it's gone!"

Rosie was impressed by Paul's news, but she felt strangely unsympathetic. Maybe it was because Paul was part of Clea's *Question Troop*. Or maybe Rosie was just starting to feel villainous. . . .

"Hmm," she whispered to Viola. "Maybe Tall Ted took it."

"Oh man!" said Sylvester, crouched on the lawn at the Four Corners. "I wish I'd been there." Viola, Rosie, and Woodrow huddled nearby as the sun descended beyond the horizon across the Hudson. After all the drama, the play rehearsal had let out early. When Viola had gotten home, she'd called an emergency meeting of the mystery club.

"Me too. That all sounds really exciting," said Woodrow.

"So what are we going to do about it?" Rosie asked.

"About what?" said Viola. "Clea or the monster?"

"Aren't they one and the same now?" said Woodrow with a smirk.

"Tall Ted and Clea Keene might indeed be monsters," Viola agreed, "but in completely different ways. Strangely, I think Ted will be easier to deal with."

"How do you figure that?" said Sylvester.

"We'll debunk Tall Ted like we've done with the other local beastly legends," said Viola, sounding as if it would be as easy as cleaning her bedroom. "Clea, on the other hand, will not be going away any time soon, especially since Rosie and I have to be in a play with her."

"But what if Tall Ted really *is* a monster?" said Sylvester.

The four friends glanced at one another. If Rosie and Viola hadn't heard the sounds coming from the school's boiler room, they might have been able to laugh off Sylvester's suggestion. As it was though, they all felt chills.

"We'll figure him out," said Viola, with a quick nod. "Easy peasy."

"In the meantime," said Woodrow brightly, pushing away the creepy mood that had followed the girls home from school, "my dad sent me an e-mail today. He heard a story down in the city he thought we might all appreciate."

*1*8

THE CASE OF THE GALLERY GRAB
(A ???? MYSTERY)

"Earlier this week, one of my dad's friends invited him to an art show at a gallery in Manhattan," said Woodrow. "A gallery is like a really small museum. My dad likes art, so he decided to check it out.

"The artist's name is Derrick Hyde. He's pretty cool. My dad attached some pictures of his artwork to the e-mail. Mr. Hyde uses plain old pencil and paper to draw realistic-looking portraits of fictional characters — Harry Potter, Frodo Baggins, Katniss Everdeen — only he makes them appear as if they're sitting for yearbook photographs."

"Those sound fun," said Sylvester. "I want to see them!"

"You and the rest of New York City," said Woodrow. "My dad said the gallery was super crowded — and hot. He wanted to step out for some air, but as he neared the door, he heard a commotion. Someone had grabbed one of Derrick's framed drawings from the wall and ran off with it."

"No way," said Sylvester.

"That's so crazy!" said Viola.

"People were shouting, 'Stop him! Stop him!'" said Woodrow. "So what did my dad do?"

"What?" asked the other three.

"He ran after the art thief . . . dressed in his business suit! He chased him down the block and managed to wrestle the picture away just as the cops showed up."

"I can't imagine your dad doing something like that," said Sylvester, not even trying to contain his amusement. He laughed loudly.

"Well, he did," said Woodrow. "The cops gave him a ride back to the gallery, where a huge crowd of photographers had gathered to watch the action. Both my father and Derrick Hyde were in the newspapers — he's sending me clippings in the mail."

"Wow," said Viola. "I bet Derrick didn't realize he was going to be so popular."

"Yeah," said Rosie. "Not every artist can say their work has been stolen from a gallery."

"True," said Sylvester, "but how many artists would really *want* their work stolen from a gallery? It sounds stressful to me!"

"Some reporters were curious about the thief," Woodrow continued, "a skinny guy named Eli Sardi. They wondered why he would attempt such a daring heist. Derrick is no Picasso — at least not yet. Eli wouldn't have gotten much money for the stolen picture. So the reporters did some research into the thief's background and discovered that Derrick and Eli both grew up in Garden City, Long Island."

"What are the chances of that?" said Rosie.

Viola raised an eyebrow in a way that suggested she didn't believe it was a coincidence. "Go on," she said to Woodrow.

"The reporters found yearbook pictures of the two boys working together in an art class. Apparently, they had been good friends."

"So Eli is an artist too?" asked Sylvester. Woodrow nodded. "Well, that might shed some light on why he tried to steal one of his old friend's drawings. Eli was probably jealous of Derrick's success!"

"Either that," said Rosie, "or he was a big fan but couldn't afford the price tag. Maybe Eli wanted something to remember Derrick by."

"Those are good theories," said Woodrow, "but there was more going on in that gallery than everyone knew."

"Like what?" asked Rosie.

"Some of the gallery patrons reported seeing Eli and Derrick chatting earlier that evening."

"Were they fighting?" said Sylvester. "Maybe Eli was mad that Derrick wouldn't give him a drawing for free."

"Nope. They weren't fighting. Supposedly, they were laughing and having a good time."

"That doesn't make any sense," said Rosie. "They're old friends. They were being social. *What made that all fall apart so quickly?*"

"Nothing," said Woodrow.

"Of course *something* had to have happened," said Viola.

"Nope. Not a thing happened that night to make their friendship fall apart," said Woodrow, with a teasing look. ***"How can that be?"***

"If nothing fell apart," said Sylvester, "then they *were* friends that night. And they're probably still friends now."

Woodrow nodded.

"That's not possible," said Rosie. "Eli *stole* the drawing. If I were Derrick, I'd be furious."

"But Derrick doesn't think like you," said Woodrow. "In fact, Derrick decided not to press charges against Eli."

"No way!" said Rosie.

Woodrow continued, ***"Why do you think Derrick would make that decision?"***

"He obviously didn't want to get his friend in trouble," said Viola.

"You're still missing something else," said Woodrow. *"Why wouldn't Derrick have wanted to get Eli in trouble for stealing a drawing from his gallery opening — a crime that got Derrick and his artwork recognized in all of the New York City newspapers?"*

"Oh my gosh," said Viola. "Of course! It was a publicity stunt!"

"A stunt?" said Sylvester. "No way."

"It had to have been," said Viola. "It all makes sense. They were seen together earlier that night. They have a history going all the way back to high school. They're still friends!"

Woodrow nodded. "Best friends who'd do anything to help get the other's work noticed. Yesterday, after all the questions from the press, Eli finally had to admit that he and Derrick had set up the heist to draw attention to the gallery show. What they didn't expect was for my father to be so close. Or to run so fast. Eli wasn't supposed to have been caught. My dad foiled their plan! At least technically . . . Derrick and Eli *are* getting all sorts of attention now. But for all the wrong reasons."

19

THE UNSAFE SAFE
(A ??? MYSTERY)

"My mom told me a story last night before bed," said Viola. "And no, it's not a fairy tale, if you were wondering." The boys laughed — obviously she'd nailed exactly what they'd been thinking. "Another strange report came in to the paper, and she wondered if I could help her figure it out. I promised to ask you guys about it, but I never got a chance today with all the Drama drama.

"Mrs. Geldman lives by herself in a great old house out on River Lane. Her husband passed away awhile ago. But she kept all of his old belongings. Her house is overstuffed with it. She recently decided to donate most of it to the Maple Avenue Church Charity Thrift Store.

"Her kids wanted to go through it first, but she said the only things she had that were valuable were in a strange old safe her husband had kept in the bedroom closet. She wasn't even sure what was locked away in there, because Mr. Geldman had neglected to give her the key. She assumed the stash was cash, or stocks, or bonds . . . bank stuff. Her kids promised to help her open the safe when they visited.

"Before her children came, Mrs. Geldman loaded up her car with a bunch of her husband's old clothes and brought them to the thrift store. The workers at the store were happy to receive such a large donation. She promised that more was on its way. She told them that she had a lot of treasures up in her old house.

"A couple days later, when Mrs. Geldman's kids came to Moon Hollow to visit, they were impressed that she'd already made some progress organizing the house. One of her sons, Melvin, went upstairs to check out the safe in the bedroom closet and to see how difficult it might be to open without the key. But when he came downstairs, he asked his mom how she'd gotten the safe open.

"Mrs. Geldman was confused. The last she'd checked, she said, the safe had been locked up tight. Everyone went upstairs to see for themselves. To their disappointment, Melvin was right. The door was open. And the safe was empty.

"An argument broke out almost immediately. Melvin's siblings believed that he had somehow broken into the safe. They thought he'd removed whatever was inside and hidden it. Melvin, of course, was insulted that his brothers and sisters would think he'd do such a thing. He wanted to prove his innocence, so he allowed them all to search his luggage and his car. No one found anything that looked like it should have been part of their inheritance.

"The family placed a police report, but so far, they haven't made any progress," said Viola. "But after thinking about the story, I told my mom that I had an idea of how someone got into the safe. *Do you guys know?*"

"Melvin didn't mention that the safe looked like it had been tampered with," said Woodrow. "So someone had to have used the key to open it." He jingled the key chain he always kept attached to his belt loop.

"You're saying the thief used the same key that Mr. Geldman had kept from his wife?" said Rosie. *"But who had gotten ahold of it?"*

"If it wasn't Melvin," said Viola, "or any of Mrs. Geldman's adult children, it had to have been someone who knew she had something valuable up in that house."

"'Treasure' was what she called it," said Sylvester.

"Oh my gosh," said Rosie. "Mrs. Geldman mentioned 'treasure' to the people at the thrift store when she dropped off her husband's old clothes."

"Exactly," said Viola. "So one of them must have gotten Mr. Geldman's key. *How?*"

"That's easy," said Woodrow. "Where do people keep keys?"

Sylvester pointed at Woodrow's waistband. "Clipped to your pants."

"True," said Woodrow. "*Or* they stick them into their pockets."

"Someone at the thrift store must have found a key ring in the pocket of one of Mrs. Geldman's donations," said Rosie.

"One of employees must have used the keys to get into her house," said Viola. "They located the safe in the closet and emptied out whatever was inside."

"Is that what you told your mom?" asked Woodrow. Viola nodded. "What's she going to do about it?"

"She already talked to the police," said Viola. "They've narrowed the suspects down to a pair of thrift store employees. Hopefully Mrs. Geldman will get her stuff back."

Rosie pressed her lips together and shook her head. "I just can't believe that someone would take advantage of a little old lady like that, especially someone who works for a charity."

"If we've learned anything this week," Viola said, "it's that monsters wear all kinds of masks. Right?"

"Yeah," said Rosie, "but how are we supposed to see through them?"

2θ

THE GLORY OF DETECTION

Over the course of the next week, the students of Moon Hollow Middle School were occupied with two recurring disturbances: more Tall Ted sightings and a thief who was targeting student belongings. Some people claimed that the two were one. Stories raced from class to class about strange growling noises coming from custodial closets, a large shadowy figure watching an outdoor soccer scrimmage from behind school windows, deep dents that had been smashed into the lockers of students who had taken stones from Purgatory Chasm. Gossip flew that Tall Ted was exacting his revenge by stealing back from those who had stolen from him. The scariest part of the whole experience was the rumor that the monster was only biding his time until he snatched a student instead of a wallet or a piece of jewelry. Everyone was frightened to walk home from school alone. Even some of the faculty were beginning to look nervous.

The Question Marks Mystery Club, however, was in detective paradise. They listened to the stories their friends told and gathered as many details as possible. Unfortunately, since the opening night of *The Villain's Web* was edging ever closer, Rosie and Viola didn't have as much time to devote to the mysteries as they would have liked. Rehearsal was eating up their freedom.

Thankfully, the play was eating Clea Keene's free time too. The Troop — as Clea and her friends had come to be known — were also trying to figure out who or what was behind the Tall Ted stories and all the stealing, without any obvious progress.

Viola, Rosie, Sylvester, and Woodrow promised one another that the Question Marks would answer the questions first. They would show these novices which of them loved mysteries more.

Viola made the mistake during one rehearsal of saying just that to Rosie while in earshot of Clea Keene and Paul Gomez.

"This isn't about a *love of mysteries*," said Clea, coming quickly to where Viola and Rosie stood offstage. "It's about stopping terror."

"Terror?" Rosie said, trying to hide her amusement.

"I'd say," Clea answered. "People are really scared. This has got to stop. Obviously, you guys are more interested in proving a point than helping your fellow students. Am I right, Paul?"

Paul Gomez came running. "Yes. Of course."

Viola sighed. "I'm sorry that you think we don't care about our 'fellow students,'" she said.

133

"Yes, solving mysteries together is like a game for us, but there's a purpose too. Our curiosity ends up helping people. We just don't go around bragging about how wonderful we are."

This seemed to sting Clea. She huffed. "That being the case . . . maybe you wouldn't mind sharing the love."

"What do you mean?" said Viola.

Clea nudged Paul, as if they had planned this little argument. He jumped, surprised, then realized it was his turn to speak. "We, uh, challenge you to solve the mystery of Tall Ted."

Rosie and Viola both blinked, speechless.

"If we solve it first," Clea added, "you have to admit that the Troop knows just as much about mysteries as you guys. In fact, you'll have to write a letter to the school paper proclaiming our . . ." She thought for a long moment. "Our glory."

"Your *glory*?" said Rosie.

"That's a little bit ridiculous," said Viola.

"And you'll have to drop out of the school play," Clea added quickly, almost under her breath.

"So that's what this is about," said Viola. "I should have known."

"What do we get if we win?" Rosie asked.

Clea sighed. "We promise to disband the Troop and stick to what we supposedly do best: acting."

"Sounds good to me," said Viola.

134

"Then we have a deal?" asked Clea.

Viola and Rosie glanced at each other. They were certain Sylvester and Woodrow would go for it. Besides, the girls were the ones who had everything to lose, the boys, not so much. But was it worth giving up their roles in the school play? They had already worked so hard. And despite all of Clea's pestering, they were having fun.

Suddenly Rosie wasn't sure what to do. But then Clea Keene raised an eyebrow, as if daring them to say no. Viola grabbed Rosie's hand.

"Deal," the girls answered at the same time.

2*1*

THE TRUTH ABOUT TALL TED
(A ?????? MYSTERY)

"So where do we start?" asked Woodrow when Rosie and Viola arrived at his house later that evening. They'd picked up Sylvester on their way over and were now sitting on the Knoxes' front steps.

Stars lit the sky over the Hudson River. In the distance, a train blew its lonely horn. The air was cool and sweet and still. "I think we need to talk to the Tall Ted witnesses," said Viola, bundling her jacket up tight. "Get a sense of what we're dealing with."

"Okay," said Sylvester. "I'll gather a list of everyone who's had a Tall Ted encounter. We can work from there."

At lunch the next day, the four found one another at their favorite table. Sylvester pulled out the notebook Viola had given him for Christmas and opened it up. He showed everyone the five names he'd written. "This is who I came up with. Does anybody have class with any of them?"

They all shook their heads no.

"But Gina Denucci volunteers in the main office during her study hall period," said Rosie, pointing at one of the names. "I could talk to her there."

"It's a start," said Viola. "The rest of us can figure out how to track down the others. Do you all want to catch up before play rehearsal? Meet outside the auditorium?"

Everyone agreed.

Rosie made her way to the main office. She noticed a skinny girl with long black hair sitting behind a desk just inside the office entrance.

"Gina?"

"Hi, Rosie," said the girl, wearing a big smile. "You need another hall pass?"

"Oh, ha, no, thanks. I was just wondering if I could ask you a couple of questions."

"About what?"

"Well . . . I heard that you might have had a Tall Ted sighting."

Gina blushed. "Oh you did, did you?" She suddenly didn't sound as outgoing as usual.

"Can you tell me a little bit about what you saw?"

Gina exhaled slowly and glanced over her shoulder. "I don't know if I should."

"Why not?"

"Some people around here don't want us talking about . . . monsters."

Rosie thought she understood. The faculty seemed to be trying to quash the spooky rumors before they got out of hand. But Rosie figured it was too late for that. "I can be quiet if you can," Rosie whispered, impressed with herself for not giving up so easily.

Gina gave another nervous glance over her shoulder, then appeared to relax slightly. "Okay," she said softly. "It was really freaky. I was here in the office after school, doing some filing for Ms. Benson, the guidance counselor, when out in the hallway I heard this weird noise."

"What did it sound like?" Rosie asked.

"Kinda gross. Like a growl mixed with . . . well, a huge burp."

Rosie crinkled her nose. "I experienced something similar near the boiler room under the stage."

Gina nodded. "When I heard it, I immediately thought of all those Tall Ted rumors. The boy I was working with that afternoon heard the noise too. We both went to the door to listen for it again. I was totally freaking out. But Thomas insisted we head toward the math wing. He thought that's where the noise had come from.

"We were halfway there when, before I knew what was happening, Thomas shouted, grabbed my hand, and pulled me back here to the office. Once I caught my breath, he asked me if I'd seen what he'd seen. I wasn't sure, but as soon as he described it, I couldn't get the image out of my head. A tall figure. Pale. Bald. With long arms and sharp claws."

"That seems to be what everyone says," said Rosie.

"Well, Thomas and I told Ms. Benson what happened. She was concerned. She went out and searched the hallway for us, but came back reporting nothing unusual. She looked at me like I'd gone crazy for seeing Tall Ted."

"But . . . according to what you just said," Rosie replied, "*you* didn't see anything. Your friend Thomas did."

Gina pursed her lips. She looked almost disappointed. "But I *almost* saw him. If I'd been looking in the right direction —" Suddenly, Gina sat up straight and glanced over Rosie's shoulder. "Oh, hi, Thomas. I was just chatting with Rosie about . . . the weather. Right, Rosie? It's been so nice out lately."

Rosie turned around to find a tall boy standing behind her. Suddenly, she felt foolish. Gina's coworker in the office was Thomas Kenyon, a member of Clea's Troop. Rosie had thought that she and Gina had been whispering so that the faculty wouldn't hear them, but she now realized she'd been wrong. Gina didn't want *Thomas* listening in. He must have asked Gina not to discuss the sighting with members of the Question Marks, since the two groups were in the midst of a mystery competition.

Thomas simply folded his arms and glared at her. Rosie took it as a sign that her business there was done.

After the last bell rang that day, Rosie found Viola, Sylvester, and Woodrow in the hallway outside of the auditorium. The girls had only a few minutes before Mrs. Glick would be expecting them inside, so Rosie lost no time relaying her experience with Gina.

"So Gina never actually saw Tall Ted?" said Sylvester.

"But Thomas did," said Woodrow. "Too bad we can't ask him about it. Being in Clea's Troop, he won't tell us a thing. Certainly nothing we could consider real evidence."

"Did you guys track down the other people on the list of witnesses?" asked Rosie.

Viola nodded. "Yeah, but their stories were similar to Gina's. They all seemed to be nearby when someone else saw something. But no one remembers who did the actual witnessing."

"What about that kid in your play?" asked Woodrow. "The one who claimed Tall Ted went into the boiler room."

"Evan Gleeson?" said Viola. "I talked to him today too. He said he *thought* he'd seen a tall shape moving in the darkness, but he couldn't be sure. Especially with the flickering lights in that hallway. Everyone's been saying that Evan saw a tall, bald figure with claws, but he was never that specific with his description."

"Weird," said Sylvester. "So we can't verify *any* eyewitness accounts?"

The other three shook their heads.

"So there's our first hint about what's really going on here," said Woodrow.

"And what would that be?" asked Sylvester.

"Without solid proof that Tall Ted exists," said Woodrow, "we have to assume that he doesn't."

"Well that's a relief," said Rosie.

"I think our next step should be to find proof that he's a fake," said Viola. "Not just a lack of proof that he's real."

"How do we do that?" asked Sylvester. "Where do we look?"

"We all know what else has been going on at the school lately," said Viola.

"The thefts?" said Woodrow. "But people are blaming those on Tall Ted too."

"So let's forget the rumors, and talk to the victims to get the facts," said Viola. "Because if Tall Ted isn't stealing people's stuff, someone else is."

A few members of the *Villain* cast headed through the auditorium doors. Rosie glanced at the clock on the wall nearby. "Viola and I have to go. But we'll catch up with you guys later this evening."

"Sylvester and I will see who we can chat with about the thefts," said Woodrow. "Have fun at rehearsal!"

That night, it was Rosie's turn to host the Question Marks. After the Smithers family dinner, the group of four gathered at the big table in the dining room.

Woodrow took a scrap of paper from his coat pocket and spread it on the table. "Sylvester and

I made some progress this afternoon," he said. "The list of names I have here are all the people who claim that Tall Ted has stolen something from them. As I understand it, only the four members of the 'Question Troop' had their homes burglarized, giving them a reason to form their group. Plus, Paul Gomez's wallet was taken from his bag in the dressing rooms under the stage, right after Evan Gleeson claimed to have seen the monster. The rest of the listed victims had their things stolen out of their lockers at school. Some of those targets had the big dents in the doors that everyone is talking about, but most of the lockers seemed to have been opened by someone with the locker combinations."

"That's bizarre," said Rosie. "How exactly would the thief get access to everyone's locker combinations?"

"Suppose Tall Ted isn't fake after all," said Sylvester, excitedly. "What if he has some sort of secret-psychic-locker-combo power?"

Woodrow nodded and smiled. "How about we keep that theory in your pocket and come back to it later?"

Sylvester scowled.

"Viola and I heard something during rehearsal this afternoon that might provide some insight into the thefts," said Rosie. "Actually, I think *this* story is scarier than anything I've heard about Tall Ted. Everyone was talking about a man who supposedly escaped from a prison upstate and has recently been seen lurking about in the Moon Hollow Hills."

"No way," said Woodrow. "My mom would have said something to me about that. She works up in those woods every day!"

"Maybe she didn't want to scare you," said Sylvester.

"It's possible that this convict is the one who's been burglarizing people's homes," said Rosie. "Could he have come into the school too?"

"That's a creepy thought," said Viola. "I'll ask my mom to look into other crime reports in the area to see if they have anything in common. Maybe we've got our culprit."

"Gosh," said Woodrow. "Now, not only do we have to deal with monsters, but we might have a dangerous criminal on our hands as well? Maybe we should just give up now. Let Clea's Troop claim the crown."

"Clea isn't any closer to an answer than we are," said Viola. "I gathered that much at rehearsal today. Anyway, the point of our contest isn't to catch a criminal . . . it's to solve the mystery. We'll leave the bounty-hunting to the proper authorities, thank you very much."

"Besides," said Rosie, "if we let Clea win, that means Viola and I have to drop out of the play. Mrs. Glick would never let us audition again."

"Then I guess it's settled," said Sylvester. "This shall be a battle to the finish."

On Friday afternoon, after Mrs. Glick assigned the *Villain* cast to their official dressing rooms, Viola and Rosie took some time to clean up and organize their spaces. The two girls even taped magazine cutouts of their favorite actresses onto their mirrors. They were happy that Clea had been placed a couple doors down from them.

They were practicing their lines, waiting for Mrs. Glick to call "places," when from down the hallway, they heard a familiar sound — one that still sent chills through their bones. It was the same growl that they'd heard a couple weeks earlier, and it was once again coming from the boiler room.

Quickly, the two peeked out the dressing room door and into the empty hallway. The sound came again, this time louder. "What do we do?" asked Rosie. All color had drained from her face.

"Investigate?" said Viola.

They held hands as they made their way toward the boiler room door. The last time they'd walked this way, they'd been surrounded by their classmates. Now, however, everyone else had apparently gone upstairs to the stage. Being alone was much creepier. When they reached the door, Viola paused, then with a deep sigh, she reached out and turned the knob. The door swung inward, and the girls peered into the darkness.

The sound came at them again, bouncing off the cinder-block walls in long echoes. Whatever was growling at them sounded as though it was just a few feet away. The girls clutched at each other, but managed not to run. "Tall Ted isn't real," Viola whispered. "So this sound can't be him."

"Then what is it?" Rosie asked.

"I have an idea. Come on. Let's see."

Rosie nearly dragged her heels as Viola pulled her through the dark doorway. This time, Viola had her key chain light in her pocket. She flicked it on. The growl rumbled again, and now that they were inside the boiler room, the girls had a better sense of where it was coming from: the great big metal furnace near the far wall.

"Is it the boiler itself making the sound?" asked Rosie. "Maybe the pipes are expanding or something?"

Viola answered by shining her light into the space between the wall and the boiler. "Aha!" she said, reaching forward to grasp the object that was lying there. "I think we've found our culprit."

"A walkie-talkie?" said Sylvester, feeling the weight of the device as Woodrow handed it to him. The group sat at the Harts' small kitchen table, passing the walkie-talkie around.

It had been two hours since the girls had left the boiler room. Mrs. Hart had made some lemonade earlier in the day, and Viola poured everyone a glass.

"But who was on the other end?" Woodrow asked.

"That's the big question," said Rosie.

"As soon as we found it," said Viola, "I picked it up and pressed the talk button. I growled back. *Grrr.*"

"You did not!" said Woodrow, laughing.

"She did too!" said Rosie. "But we got no answer. In fact, the static sound that had been coming from the speaker went silent. Whoever had the other walkie-talkie must have turned it off."

"So they know they've been found out," said Sylvester. "The walkie-talkie is our proof that Tall Ted actually *is* fake. You guys, we won the contest!"

"Not quite," said Viola, taking the device back from him. "We may have proof that someone wants the students at Moon Hollow Middle School to believe we're being tormented by a monster, but we still don't know who it is. *That's* the mystery we need to solve."

Sylvester took a large swig of his lemonade. After wiping his mouth, he said, "Maybe we can have the walkie-talkie dusted for prints. If that escaped convict is the one pretending to be the monster, his fingerprints are probably on file in some sort of police database. Woodrow, doesn't your dad have connections?"

"He does," said Woodrow. "But I doubt the police will be able to pull a print off of this thing. I mean, we've been passing it around, so *our* fingerprints are all over it. Plus, Sylvester, you just wiped it on your sleeve."

"I did?" said Sylvester. "Oops."

"We're closer than ever," said Viola. "More important, we're closer than Clea. We only have a little bit further to go. We just need to figure out the next step. Speaking of which, my mom hasn't had time to look into a list of local crimes. As soon as she does that, we can look for connections between them."

"I have an idea," said Woodrow. "Kyle Krupnik mentioned that a bunch of kids from our class are meeting at the school tomorrow morning and riding their bikes up to Purgatory Chasm. They think that if they return the stones they took, all of this monster nonsense will stop. Maybe we should tag along with them and see if we come across any more clues."

"But didn't you tell Kyle what we're up to?" Viola asked. "Our classmates don't need to ride up to Purgatory with their supposedly 'stolen' stones if all they're trying to do is remove a curse that doesn't even exist."

"I did tell Kyle that he has nothing to be

148

scared of," said Woodrow. "But I think it's all gone too far at this point. Nobody knows what to believe anymore."

"Well, I'm in," said Rosie.

"Me too," said Sylvester.

"And me," said Viola, "of course."

"Great," said Woodrow. "We can ride to the school together."

"I'll need help pumping up my bike tires," Rosie added. "I haven't gone that far since last fall."

It was a lovely spring morning — the dreamy kind of Saturday that tells a story of changing seasons. Birds were chattering loudly outside bedroom windows, waking and annoying late sleepers. The smell of cut grass lingered in the air. You could almost hear the Hudson River down the hill flowing along its ancient channel toward the Atlantic Ocean. The day was perfect for solving mysteries.

In the school parking lot, the sun provided warmth against the crisp breeze. Viola, Rosie, Sylvester, and Woodrow stood beside their bikes and watched as more and more of their classmates rode up the long drive to the school's entrance.

Kyle Krupnik approached them, patting his jacket pocket. "I can't wait to get rid of this thing," he said.

The four knew he was referring to his Purgatory stone. They'd agreed to let their friends believe what they needed to in order to feel safe again. "Us too," said Woodrow, pointing at his backpack.

"Oh my gosh," said Rosie, looking over Kyle's shoulder. "What are *they* doing here?"

Clea Keene was pedaling up the school's driveway on a shiny pink bike. Rainbow streamers fluttered from her handlebars. Paul Gomez, Thomas Kenyon, and Shanti Lane followed close behind her on their own bikes.

"They must have had the same idea as us," said Viola. "I guess I should stop underestimating them."

A few minutes later, nearly twenty bikers set off together into the Moon Hollow Hills, winding their way up the road toward Purgatory Chasm, growing winded with each sharp turn. The Question Marks kept clear of Clea's Troop. They wanted to stay on task and decided that to invite conversation might only provide distraction. Strangely, the Troop must have had the same idea, because Clea and her crew barely even glanced at the original mysterious four. It made Viola wary. What did Clea have up her sleeve?

When they finally reached the park and chained their bicycles to a wobbly wooden fence, everyone headed down the path toward the chasm's steep cliffs. To Viola's surprise, Clea rushed forward and held up her hands, stopping the group just before the two large boulders that marked Purgatory's entrance.

"My older brother told me that the best way to keep Tall Ted from returning," she announced, "is to place your stolen stone back in the location from which you took it." A collective groan rose from the group, and Clea raised her hands even higher. "It doesn't have to be perfect. The stones just have to be close. In other words, if you all just drop your stones *right here*, it won't do any good." Clea turned toward the shadowy ravine. "That's where you'll want to go. Down. Deep." She took the first step. Everyone followed.

Since Viola, Rosie, Sylvester, and Woodrow were near the back of the group, they were the last to cross the chasm's threshold. Once they did, they could sense the tension of their classmates, who were trying to remember the spots they'd picked up their stones. While trudging along, the four all tried to ask their friends about their recent experiences. Had anything else been stolen? Had they noticed any suspicious people since the Tall Ted rumors had begun? But no one was interested in talking. Viola began to worry that this trip wasn't going to help the case at all.

When they finally made their way to the bottom of the ravine, the Question Marks regrouped. "What do we do now?" asked Rosie. "We've come to a dead end." Already, their classmates had begun the ascent back up the wooded path beside the chasm. Even though the sky above was crystal clear, the bare branches cast spidery shadows upon everything, creating an odd twilight effect in the deep woods. It made sense that Tall Ted's story was connected to this place. This would have been a perfect home for a hideous creature trying to hide from society. Or for an escaped prisoner on the run. But would either one leave the safety of the hills to torment a bunch of middle-schoolers?

There must have been more to the story. But what kind of story was it: a hard-boiled true-crime tale or a monstrous chiller-thriller?

"Whatever we do," said Woodrow, "we should do it quickly. I don't really want to be left behind."

"Me neither," said Sylvester.

"We're not the last ones," said Viola, heading toward a dark space at the base of one of the cliffs. A wooden post had been stuck in the dirt nearby. It read: *The Devil's Armpit.* "Look." Bending down, she pulled a backpack out from behind a small rock. "Someone else is still down here with us."

"Hello?" Woodrow called out. His voice echoed all around them, hanging in the air for what seemed like an extremely long time. But no one and nothing answered.

"Let's go," said Sylvester. "I've got a bad feeling."

"If this bag belongs to one of our friends," said Viola, "we can't leave them here." The other three looked troubled as the shadows and cliffs started to work at their imaginations too. Viola shook her head, then opened the backpack. Inside, she found an apple, a pastel-colored teen-romance novel, and a small spiral notebook. She pulled out the notebook and opened the cover. It was blank. When she examined the novel, she noticed a name written on the first page — Shanti Lane. "It's the Troop," said Viola. "They're still here."

"What are they up to?" Rosie asked.

"Maybe they've made a discovery," said Sylvester.

"Can I see that?" Woodrow asked, reaching for the notebook. Viola handed it over. After brushing his fingers against the blank first page, he glanced at the rest of them. "I think I've made a discovery too. This notebook tells us exactly where Clea's Troop went." He nodded at the dark space at the bottom of the cliff. It was just tall enough for someone to crawl inside on their hands and knees.

"How did a blank piece of paper clue you in?" asked Sylvester, looking like he didn't want to know the answer.

153

Woodrow held up the notebook. "The first page has been torn out. But Shanti's pen mark left an impression on the second page. Look closely and you can see that she wrote down *'The Devil's Armpit'*." He pointed at the dark space. "She also drew what appears to be a map of the cave. She probably copied it from the Moon Hollow Hills Park website."

"Do you think the entire Troop went in there?" asked Rosie, hugging her arms across her chest. "Why would they do that?"

"They must be looking for something," said Sylvester.

"What are we waiting for?" said Viola, taking back Shanti's notebook. Pulling a pencil from her own backpack, she carefully rubbed the graphite over the impression Shanti had left on the notebook's second page. Shanti's drawing stood out white against the gray. "We've got their map now. Let's see if we can learn what they already know."

"You want us to follow them?" said Sylvester. "Is it dangerous?"

Woodrow nodded at the Devil's Armpit sign. "This is a ranger marker. If we stick to the route the park mapped out, we should be fine."

"Should be?" said Sylvester.

"Come on," said Viola, tightening her bag straps against her shoulders and peering beyond the jagged mouth of rock. "There's no way I'm going to let them win."

The entry was tight, but after a few feet, the ceiling of rock expanded enough so that the four could all stand comfortably. Dim light filtered in through the cave mouth behind them, barely bright enough for the group to make out one another's faces. Luckily, Viola's key chain light still had enough battery power to illuminate the map. When she shined it at the walls, another ominous entry revealed itself just ahead. "This way," she said, squeezing into the passage, heading toward the darkened depths. The other three reluctantly followed.

The smell of damp earth was mixed with another strong, nearly overpowering scent. Sylvester gagged as he got a good whiff of it. But the stench was the least of their concerns.

With every twist of the cavern, the group knew they were moving farther away from the light of day and closer to some great unknown. The history of the place was almost tangible, like you could breathe it in and suddenly know more than you did before.

After coming through one particularly tight squeeze, Sylvester, who was trailing the rest, yelped. "Something dripped on my neck."

"Bat droppings, probably," Woodrow said.

"There are bats in here?"

"It was water, silly," said Rosie. "Look, we're practically walking through a stream of it." Viola shined the light at their feet, revealing a small trickle of moisture that followed them deeper into the earth. "How much farther, Viola?" Rosie asked.

"I'm not sure," said Viola. "There's nothing on Shanti's map that says where the Troop was going to stop."

"Shh," said Woodrow. "Listen."

Sure enough, they all heard voices, whispering from somewhere ahead. Viola turned off her flashlight. In the distance, light glowed dimly. "I think we found them," she whispered as quietly as she could. "Come on."

The four treaded softly, trying to keep their presence a secret from the Question Troop. The light ahead grew brighter. They were almost upon Clea and her friends when there was a flash and they were blinded. None of them had a chance to cry out before another flash lit the tunnel. It was immediately obvious that someone up ahead had just taken a picture.

"A little warning would have been nice," came Paul Gomez's voice from around the bend.

"Sorry," said Thomas Kenyon. "Just doing my job."

"Have we got it, then?" said Clea. "The proof we came for?"

"Seems good to me," came another girl's voice. Shanti Lane.

Clea shushed them. After a second, she said, "I thought I heard something."

Before any of the Question Marks could move, a beam of light was shining upon them.

"I should have known," said Clea, peering at them. "We've been followed."

"Oh no," said Shanti. "I forgot my bag at the entrance of the cave."

"Nice," said Clea, turning away. "You tipped them off."

"Sorry," said Shanti.

With their own cover blown, Viola led her group into the space where the Troop had gathered. This new cavern was about the size of her bedroom, and it seemed to be just as cluttered. The tunnel continued into the opposite wall, but it had been blocked off by a single metal bar cemented into the stone. It was the Park Service's way of telling would-be explorers *Do Not Enter*. But that wasn't what captured the Question Marks' attention.

Illuminated by the other group's bright lights, the cave was filled with several satchels, a sleeping bag, and piles of half-eaten food. A few fast-food burger wrappers had been tossed haphazardly around.

Someone had been living in here.

"What is all this stuff?" asked Woodrow.

"What's it look like?" said Clea. "A camp. We've discovered the secret of Tall Ted. Sorry to say, we beat you to the prize, kids."

"I don't get it," said Rosie, still unsure of what she was looking at. "What exactly is the secret?"

Viola wandered through the site, peering closely at the strewn detritus. Bending down, she lifted what appeared to be a pale rubber mask from the dirty sleeping bag. The mask was the head of a strange, bald creature, with dark, deep-set eyes. The mask looked like something out of a horror movie. Tall Ted?

"Isn't it obvious?" said Clea. "We found the lair of the thief who's been terrorizing the students of Moon Hollow Middle School."

Woodrow peeked into one of the satchels. "She's right," he said. "This looks like the stolen stuff." He reached into the bag and pulled out a couple of wallets.

"And check this out!" said Viola. Underneath the monster mask, she'd located an even more revealing clue: the twin of the walkie-talkie they'd found in the boiler room. "I guess this pretty much settles it." Viola looked so disappointed, Rosie thought she might have been on the verge of tears. "They're right. Whoever set up this camp is the guilty one. The thief was masquerading as Tall Ted, scaring students, then taking their stuff while they were distracted. Isn't that what happened to Paul in the dressing room when we heard the growling sound near the boiler?"

Paul perked up, then nodded enthusiastically.

"So then . . . who is it?" Sylvester asked. "Who is the thief?"

"We think it's the escaped convict everyone is talking about," said Paul excitedly. Clea threw him a threatening glance. It was obvious that she felt this was her story to tell.

"The convict has been hiding out here?" Rosie asked, glancing around. "What if he comes back?"

"He just might," said Clea. "That's why we should probably get going." She nodded at her Troop and they stood at attention, like loyal subjects.

"Wait a second," said Viola. "How did you figure out the convict's hiding place was up here at Purgatory Chasm?"

Clea paused, as if gathering her thoughts. "We . . . followed clues. We don't have to tell you what they were. That wasn't part of the rules."

Viola, Rosie, Sylvester, and Woodrow glanced at one another skeptically.

"That's true," said Woodrow. "But we followed some clues too. And our clues indicate that you four are lying."

"Lying?" Clea's ice-blue eyes widened. She scoffed. "We are not lying. We've just uncovered the biggest scandal Moon Hollow has ever seen.

We're gonna be heroes as soon as we tell the police what we've found. I'd be surprised if they don't give us a medal."

"A medal?" said Woodrow, amused. "Really?"

"Why wouldn't they?" said Clea, her anger building. Her friends looked nervous, but the rest of the Question Marks only looked confused.

Still, Woodrow continued. "Because as soon as you mention an escaped convict to them, they'll laugh in your face. *Don't you know why?*"

Clea didn't answer. She only stood there, looking defeated. So Viola spoke up instead. "Being a lawyer down in New York City, Woodrow's dad has connections to the state police. I'm guessing Mr. Knox did some checking up," Viola said hopefully.

Woodrow nodded.

"There haven't been any recent prison breaks upstate, have there?" Rosie asked.

"Nope," said Woodrow. "So that leaves the question . . . whose lair is this?"

"It must still belong to the thief," said Sylvester. "Here's all the loot."

"Exactly," said Rosie, as an idea struck her. "The loot that was stolen from the lockers. Lockers that were not broken into. A seemingly impossible task. Unless the thief had access to locker combinations. I know someone like that. ***Don't you guys?***"

"Gina Denucci!" said Sylvester. "She volunteers in the office. She must know where the locker combination files are stored!"

"She might," said Rosie. "But I was thinking about someone else. In fact, this other person happened to be one of the thief's victims."

"Thomas," Woodrow said with a smile. "You work with Gina, don't you?"

Even in the warm flashlight glow, Thomas's face blushed almost purple. "I do, but —"

"Don't say another word," Clea interrupted.

"Why not?" said Viola. "Don't want to incriminate yourselves?" Every member of the Troop all stared at their feet, except for Clea. She looked defiantly into Viola's eyes. "It all makes sense," Viola continued. "You four were the first victims of the robberies. In fact, that's what supposedly brought you together — the fact that someone had stolen from you. You formed your 'troop' in order to catch the thief. But what if you stole from yourselves to make it *seem* like you were victims? You were all friends before any of this started, weren't you?"

"Like we'd really do that," said Clea, with a smirk. "Steal from ourselves? Ha!"

"I think you would," said Rosie. "You do have a fondness for storytelling, Clea. Remember the Lady in Green?"

"That stuff really happened!" Clea insisted. "Everyone knows about her."

"Just like everyone knew about the legend of Tall Ted?" said Sylvester. "If I remember correctly, it was you who told the story on the bus ride after the field trip. You also planted the thought that whoever took a stone from Purgatory Chasm should watch out — the monster would come after them."

"It did the trick," said Woodrow. "Everyone at school has been jumping at shadows for the past few weeks. But no one's actually *seen* a monster — except for you, Thomas. Of course, no one would realize you'd lied if the thief left behind a Tall Ted mask. Were you the one doing the walkie-talkie growls too?"

Thomas cleared his throat, but said nothing.

"A little paranoia works wonders when you're trying to manipulate people," said Rosie.

"Speaking of which," said Viola, "where did the rumors of the escaped convict begin? I first heard about him during play rehearsal. Did you start that one too, Clea?" Clea remained stone-faced. "You needed to tie the legend of Tall Ted to a real-life thief, someone you could blame, someone you could reveal as the true villain at the center of the web. That's why you're up here, taking pictures. When the truth is, Clea, you're the villain. As obvious as it now seems, you did a pretty good job of tricking all of us."

"Gosh," said Rosie, shaking her head, "who knew the lengths you'd go to just to get us to drop out of the play? You assumed Mrs. Glick would give you one of our parts?"

"You can't prove any of this," said Clea, stepping closer to her friends. "Come on, you guys. Let's get out of here."

"We'll make sure this gets back into the right hands," said Sylvester, picking up the satchel of loot.

Clea grabbed Paul's wrist and began to pull him toward the tunnel from which the Question Marks had come. Thomas and Shanti shuffled along behind them. They disappeared through the natural doorway, taking their flashlights with them.

A few seconds went by before Viola remembered to click on her own key chain light. "I guess we should —" she began, but she was interrupted by a tremendous roar that echoed through the cavern. This was followed by sounds of wild screaming. The Question Marks froze, wide-eyed in the cold blue light.

Through the tunnel entrance, they watched flashlight beams bob as the Troop ran back toward the fake campsite. Clea and her friends burst into the room, wearing looks of pure terror. "Help us!" she shouted. "Something's up there."

"We heard," said Rosie, trying to control the shaking of her own voice. "Did you see what it was?"

164

"I saw a large shadow coming toward us," said Shanti. "After that, we all just turned and ran."

"Tall Ted is real," whispered Sylvester, sounding half-pleased and half-horrified at his realization. They all moved away from the mouth of the tunnel.

"We'll worry about that some other time," said Woodrow. "Right now, we have to find a way out of here."

"We can't go back in that direction," said Paul. "The creature's waiting."

"But that's the way out," said Clea. "What are we supposed to do?"

They had no time to answer. The sound of something sharp scraping against stone echoed through the passage. Whatever the Troop had seen had followed them. If they didn't make a move, and soon, they would come face-to-face with a true Purgatory beast.

"This way," said Woodrow, pulling Viola and her key chain light toward the opposite wall — the one with the barred-off hole that led to who knew where. No one argued. All eight of them were suddenly a single unit, leaping the bar one at time, then moving deeper into the darkness of the cave system.

They shuffled away as quickly as they could, slipping and sliding through the damp labyrinth, trying to put as much distance as possible

165

between themselves and the creature on their tail. After several minutes of barreling through the darkness, with nothing but shaky flashlights to guide their way, they paused. Listening carefully, none of them heard anything except a soft trickle of underground water flowing somewhere nearby.

"Are we safe?" whispered Clea.

"From the beast?" said Woodrow. "I'd say yes. But from the darkness, I'm not so sure. Was anyone paying attention to the direction we were running?"

Everyone shook their heads.

"Oh my gosh," said Shanti. "How are we going to find our way back? My map doesn't cover this part of the cave."

"We're lost," said Sylvester. "Lost and doomed."

Viola rolled her eyes. "And to think I once promised myself I'd never die in a cave with a bunch of drama queens."

"I'm pretty sure I can get us out of here," said Rosie. "And we won't even have to backtrack."

"How are you gonna do that?" asked Clea, with a sneer. "Are you suddenly psychic?"

"No," said Rosie. "But there's something in these caverns that can tell us which direction to go. And it's not a monster, if you were wondering. I bet my friends know what it is. *Right, guys?*"

Everyone thought about Rosie's question for several seconds, as if their lives depended on it — a good thing, because that was in fact the case.

"Is it the sound of the running water?" asked Paul shyly.

"Yup," said Rosie. "If we can find the underground stream that's making that constant noise, it might just lead us out of here."

It took the group another few minutes and a few U-turns to find the bubbling brook. The water flowed smoothly through a deep cut in the rock. Rosie led the way, following the stream when possible. Every now and again, she'd lose direction as the water disappeared into a crevice. When that happened, however, she would listen carefully, and pick up the path in another tunnel. The others listened for different kinds of sounds, like the one that had originally sent them running.

They had been walking for what seemed like forever, and though Sylvester was thankful that nothing was pursuing them — he hoped! — he wondered how much farther down they could travel. Shouldn't they start to head upward eventually? Wasn't that where light would be?

Seconds later, Rosie cried out, "Listen!" The sound of rushing water was growing louder and louder with every step they took. "I think we're almost there."

"Where?" asked Sylvester.

"The Hudson!"

Of course, Sylvester thought. Purgatory Chasm was so high up in the Moon Hollow Hills that their descent through the caves had brought them down closer to the large river's edge. They could see light up ahead cascading toward them like a fountain. Soon, the mouth of the cave appeared.

As the group made their way out into the woods by the river, they shouted with relief. The sun hung low in the sky, over the trees across the water. They jumped up and down, spiraling in a circle, like kindergartners playing ring-around-the-rosy at recess. Viola, Rosie, Sylvester, and Woodrow had never felt so happy. Yes, they'd solved the mystery of Tall Ted and the middle school thief. But really . . . did that even matter anymore? They were alive and they let the woods know it!

"Arroooo!" they howled together.

After the celebration, Thomas spoke up. "How are we supposed to get back up to our bikes?"

"Who the heck cares?" said Rosie, bursting out with a roar of laughter. Her friends soon joined in, reveling in the pure joy of the spring sunlight.

Together, covered in dirt, dust, and grime, they trod along the riverbank, stepping through weeds, dead leaves, and an abundance of mud.

They knew that the water would lead them back to town and civilization before sunset. They also knew they'd have to answer to their parents for what had happened, but even the thought of that was more appealing than getting forever lost in the monstrous caves underneath Purgatory.

When they reached the train station on Oakwood Avenue, the Question Marks split off from the Troop and headed up toward their own neighborhood, chatting the entire way. Just before they reached the comforting familiarity of their block, Sylvester asked a question that he knew would haunt him for a long time if he didn't learn the answer. "What was it that roared at us in the caves?" he said. "Does anyone have an idea?"

"Oh, that?" said Rosie. "Simple. It was a bear."

"No way," said Woodrow, his skin erupting in gooseflesh. "We were almost eaten by a bear?"

"That's no joke," said Viola. "We've all heard about the animals up in the Moon Hollow Hills. Sure, what Clea's Troop described sounds like it could have been a bear. Is that what clued you in?" Rosie shook her head. ***"Then how can you be sure what we heard was a bear?"***

"Do you guys remember that stench we smelled when we first entered the cave?" Rosie asked. They nodded. "I knew it wasn't merely dirt. I watched my step as we went farther along. I noticed some large droppings, and I instantly knew what kind of danger we might have been dealing with."

"And you didn't turn us around right then?" asked Woodrow.

"I couldn't," said Rosie. "We needed to find Clea, Paul, Thomas, and Shanti. Yes, we had a mystery to solve. But we also had to make sure that our classmates would end up safe at the end of the day. I bet it was all those burger wrappers that lured the poor thing into the Devil's Armpit. Unfortunately, the bear encountered us instead. We probably scared it as much as it scared us."

"You just keep telling yourself that," said Sylvester.

The four stepped onto the lawn that made up each of their backyards. Wandering to the center, Sylvester dropped the satchel he'd carried from the cave. Exhausted, the rest of them plopped down onto the grass at the Four Corners.

A minute later, Sylvester started giggling.

"What's up?" Woodrow asked.

Trying to control himself, Sylvester answered, "I think that's the first time bear poop has been a clue in one of our mysteries!"

"Ew!" said Viola. "Hopefully, it will be the last time too!"

22

BULLIES, VILLAINS, MONSTERS, AND THIEVES

A few weeks later, *The Villain's Web* opened to a standing ovation in the Moon Hollow Middle School auditorium. The entire cast was ecstatic with the reception. They'd worked hard, and afterward Mrs. Glick assured them that they had deserved all of the applause.

Rosie was proud that she'd gotten through the performance without a single stomach cramp. And Viola was happy that after everything that had occurred up in the Moon Hollow Woods, Clea finally allowed her to be the true villain, as she'd been cast.

On the Monday after the Purgatory escape, the Question Marks had turned the loot in to Principal Dzielski. She asked them where they had gotten it, and the group told her the same story they'd told their parents: the truth. Later, Clea, Thomas, Paul, and Shanti were called into the office to give their own version of the tale. Unfortunately for Clea, Thomas cracked, admitting that he'd taken locker combinations from the office files. Principal Dzielski doled out her usual punishment. The Troop would spend the next week and a half in detention.

Clea begged Mrs. Glick to allow her to stay in the play. The director agreed, but only once Clea promised to keep the drama onstage, where it belonged.

"So, do you think you'll audition again next year?" Woodrow asked the girls.

The four friends had nabbed the corner booth at the Main Street Diner after the show finished. Their parents had squeezed into the booth behind them and were chatting about how impressed they were with the middle school's production.

The rest of the diner was crowded, as it usually was after a school function. Woodrow thought he saw Mickey Molynew sitting at a booth near the back with someone who could have been his father. Was it possible that Mickey had waved at him? It was difficult to be sure, but Woodrow thought it was nice to imagine.

Several small children ran up the aisle near the long counter wearing pale, bald monster masks. The party supply store around the corner had recently sold out of what had become known as the Tall Ted Special.

After word spread about what had gone down at Purgatory Chasm, the town had collectively shuddered that some of its own children had been capable of wreaking such havoc, but they also secretly breathed a sigh of relief.

Sometimes even grown-ups need reminding that there are no such thing as monsters.

"I'm not sure if I'll stay in drama club," said Viola. "I feel like I should try something new."

"Well, I'm definitely going to do it again," said Rosie. "Hopefully, next time Mrs. Glick won't choose a melodrama though. All that villainy was kind of overwhelming. I realized that I don't like playing a victim."

"I didn't think of you that way," said Sylvester. "You totally put Viola in her place."

"Don't you mean *her character* put *my character* in her place?" said Viola, raising an eyebrow.

"Oh. Yeah. Right."

"Well, it sure felt great to watch the good guys finally win," said Woodrow. "I think that was my favorite part of the whole thing. The ending."

"Absolutely," said Rosie, popping a french fry in her mouth. "But everybody knows that all the fun is in getting there."

ABOUT THE AUTHOR

Dan Poblocki is the author of *The Stone Child* and *The Nightmarys*. Like many writers, he's had a long list of strange jobs. Dan has traveled New Jersey as a bathing suit salesman, played the role of Ichabod Crane in a national tour of *The Legend of Sleepy Hollow*, wrangled the audience for *Who Wants to Be a Millionaire?*, sold snacks at *The Lion King*'s theater on Broadway, recommended books at Barnes & Noble, answered phones for Columbia University, and done research at Memorial Sloan-Kettering Cancer Center. He has never been a detective though, and after writing the Mysterious Four books, he thinks he might just give it a try.

Visit the author at www.danpoblocki.com.